THE HELL'S HALF ACRE CHASE

CHASE

DARIA MIGOUNOVA

MAVERICK
PRODUCTIONS INC.

Part 1 of the St. Isidore Series

"Attention to detail; commitment to quality." -- Niagara Co.

ACKNOWLEDGMENTS

My gratitude to my husband Boris, the first reader (technically listener) of this novel and relentless fan. Thank you for your endless support and for your sports knowledge. Special thanks to my one of my oldest friends, Deborah-Lynn, with whom I've concocted this tale many years ago. This story would not exist without your contributions and I sincerely hope you enjoy the final version. Finally, a huge thank you to my family for encouraging me and being the fearless early readers of this novel.

ONE

NOVEMBER

- Toronto, Canada. September 2, 2013 -

Noa absentmindedly toyed with the rim of his paper cup, silently observing the patrons of the coffee shop in the lobby of the Canadian Security Intelligence Service Headquarters. It was about 8:30 in the morning – still early, but the shop was crowded. The din of the breakfast rush filled him with the sense of dread that he usually got in busy places.

Setting the ruined cup aside, Noa pulled out his phone to start up a game of Tetris, frustrated that he couldn't simply have a cigarette instead. While playing the game he played a thousand times before, his eyes never stopped scanning the crowd.

Granted, Noa looked a little out of place.

Among the sea of briefcases, high heels and ties, the teenager in a hoodie, playing with his cellphone in front of a half-eaten donut, looked like he took a wrong turn from the subway. But aside from a couple of sideways glances, no one seemed to pay him any attention.

He swiped down a T-shape to clear another level.

Shouldn't be long now, he thought, stuffing the remnants of his breakfast into an old backpack and pulling the hood of his sweater over his messy hair.

At about a quarter to 9:00, Noa laid eyes on his targets.

A man with dark hair in a black suit and woman with a russet bun in a grey blazer joined the coffee shop line-up. They were too caught up in their conversation to notice the teenager join their queue a few people behind them.

"—had to push out my ten o'clock to tomorrow, which screwed up my lunch plans at *Momofuku*." The woman was ranting to her colleague, slight French accent and heavy irritation in her words. She pulled her cellphone out of a large purse, skimming her calendar.

The badge on her blazer read *Lavoie, Miriam | Intelligence Officer, Financial Crime.*

"I tried to get us out of it, Miriam. But Priya from HR said it *had* to be today. Those orders came from the top, apparently." The man in the suit was a bit younger than his associate but held an air of calm in contrast to her irritability. The badge hanging off his belt read *Koven, Alexander | Intelligence Officer, Cybercrime.*

Agent Lavoie peered over the shoulder of the woman in front of her, crossing her arms. "Why couldn't 'Priya from HR' conduct the interview? Don't we have enough to do? God knows I do, with that Niagara case."

Agent Koven raised an eyebrow. "I do too, you know. I just took over the cybersecurity portfolio, and it's a mess. There are maybe two and a half competent people on that team." Then he shrugged, "Maybe that's why they're sending us that kid?"

Lavoie laughed harshly. "I hope you're being sarcastic, Alex. Do you know how many applicants we get each year? You think a child is what we need? It's insulting."

They reached the front of the line.

"Regardless, we have to interview him to appease the execs, so – hi, large black and breakfast wrap please, thanks – so we might as well get it over with quickly," said Koven.

"Medium non-fat soy latte, thanks." Lavoie shook her head, "I'm complaining to someone about this. Once I figure out who arranged it. I hate kids. Especially entitled ones."

As the barista read the agents their totals, Noa quietly slipped out of the line. He put his phone to his ear, pretending to get a call.

"Entitled?" Koven echoed, pulling his phone out. "Oh, I'll use Apple Pay," he motioned it to the barista.

Lavoie held her phone out too, opening the shop's mobile app. "You know, this fancy collegiate or whatever. St. Isidore's. A few great placements here and there, and they think their reputation is good enough to send kids to international agencies. Ridiculous."

"Mm. Perhaps."

Uncomfortably weaving through neighboring caffeine addicts, Noa hesitated for a lingering moment by the register where the agents were paying for their coffees. He tapped a few buttons on his phone, and then slipped it into his pocket. Based on the models, they were using corporate mobiles. As they auto connected to the coffee shop Wi-Fi to pay, Noa couldn't ask for a better angle.

After a few seconds, he disappeared into the crowd and headed to the elevators.

Noa ducked behind a group of nearly identical-looking businessmen, avoiding the eyes of a security guard, and shuffled into an open lift. He swiped a visitors' badge on the scanner, much to the surprise of a few other riders, and rode up in silence to the 18th floor.

Minutes later, agents Koven and Lavoie would also

arrive at the 18th floor, leaving a shared elevator. But Noa had already snuck into the bathroom, locked himself in a stall, and got to work.

One hour left until 10:00am. Plenty of time.

Noa hung up his old backpack on the stall's hook and took out a compact laptop, powering it on. With a cable that he dug out from his pocket, he connected his cellphone, as well as another cube-shaped device that had an 11 engraved on its side.

As he worked, Noa played back the conversation he overheard earlier in his mind. He frowned. Then he smirked. Then he grinned and started humming the Tetris *Korobeiniki* tune to himself.

Ten minutes remaining.

Noa ejected the cables and cube from the laptop, put everything back into his bag, and pulled out a suit jacket. It was un-ironed and about two sizes too big, but it would have to do. He switched the hoodie for the jacket and examined himself in the mirror.

Atop his head was a mop of messy red hair, still tousled from the hood of his sweater. The bags under his tired deep green eyes were barely obscured by black-rimmed glasses, which framed an overall thin teenage face dusted with freckles.

The sleeves of the jacket extended over his wrists, making Noa appear even younger than he was. He rolled them up once, which looked a bit silly, but at least gave some semblance of age. He shrugged, giving up on his attempt to fix his hair. *It's not like they're gonna take me seriously.*

5 minutes remaining. Noa slung his backpack over his shoulder and left the bathroom, heading down the hall to the main boardroom. Through the closed door, he could

hear the faint voices of agents Koven and Lavoie inside and fought to suppress a smile.

At 10:01, Agent Koven opened the door. Noa stood.

"Hey there," Koven said with a gentle smile. "Noa Sinclair?"

Noa smiled back, "That's me."

TWO

RAINBOW BRIDGE

- Niagara Falls, US Border. September 2, 2013 -

Traffic inched along slowly over the grand Niagara River. Autumn was on its way, bringing with it thousands of tourists, eager to behold the so-called Eighth Wonder of the World.

Packed sedans and minivans lined the Rainbow International Bridge bumper-to-bumper, cracking their windows open to get a whiff of the cool, misty breeze drifting down from the falls. Children stuck their heads out of car windows, hoping to catch a glimpse of an actual rainbow manifesting over the river.

Besides the passenger vehicles, a couple of trucks contributed to the congestion on the bridge. Upon reaching the state line tollgate, the Border Protection Officer would gesture for the truck driver to roll down their window.

"Are you aware that commercial trucks are not permitted on Rainbow Bridge, sir?"

"Well, good day to you too, then! Beautiful day, 'innit?" The driver of this particular truck smiled, tipping his baseball cap in faux courtesy. The sides of the cargo trailer were white, as if recently painted over.

The officer did not return the small talk. "Trucks are supposed to take the Lewiston Bridge, sir. Do you have authorization to be on this route?"

"Sure do, my friend." The driver adjusted the cap on his head and smiled again, confidently. "This here's a fresh shipment of ice wines, made out to order for the Niagara Co. Had to drive real far to get here. Shame to turn back now."

"Niagara Co." The officer eyed the truck's blank exterior, then the driver's unnerving grin. "I see."

"First day?" The truck driver suddenly laughed, startling the officer enough to reach for his gun. "No, no need for that, friend. You'll get used to us; you'll see. Now go on, be a good boy and let me through."

On edge but ultimately defeated, the officer opened the toll gate for the truck.

"Oh and, since we're buds now, I'll give you a heads up that another shipment's right behind me. Good day to ya!" The trucker smiled once more, driving onto United States soil.

The officer sat in his booth nervously for the next hour or so, until another commercial truck rolled up to the gate. This one had fading advertisements on display, particularly for ice cream sundaes.

"Hello," the officer said as the truck's driver looked at him expectantly. "Are you aware that cargo and commercial trucks are not permitted on Rainbow Bridge?"

"Ah," the driver mouthed, almost noiselessly. "Okay. I has cargo that needs crossing, yes?" He had a thick Eastern European accent but spoke with the patience of a father explaining arithmetic to a small child. "Is important cargo."

"Commercial trucks can use the Lewiston—"

"No, you are not understand," the driver shook his head. "Is important cargo, *very important*. Ice cream, yes? You like ice cream?"

The border officer sputtered. "You're delivering ice cream?"

"Yes! Yes, ice cream. Niagara Company, special delivery. Ice cream, how you say, melting? You understanding me now?"

"Niagara Company." That name again. "I think I do," the officer said, not bothering to hide his disapproval. "Fine, go on."

"Good man." The driver gave him a brief nod as a sign of thanks and passed through the border.

After a few minutes, the truck made a sharp right onto 1st Street from the main road, slowing near the intersection of 1st and Old Falls Street. Between the hotels, museums and restaurants, the truck maneuvered its way behind an ice cream shop, whose façade read *The Polar Parlor*.

As the driver parked and got out of the truck, he was greeted by an energetic young woman in an apron that matched the shop's design.

"Sergey! How're you doin', sugar?" She gave him a hug, patting his back. "You're late!"

With a hidden blush, he cleared his throat. "Yes, sorry Miss Elli. Is new border guard, he give me trouble. Ask lots of questions."

"Trouble?" Elli stepped back, placing her hands on her hips in an exaggerated way. "That won't do. I'll get that all sorted for you with the Boss hon', don't worry." She clasped her hands together, curly blonde locks bouncing with the motion. "Now let's see what you brought – I don't have much time."

"Of course, yes," Sergey nodded, hurrying to the back of the truck with Elli close behind.

While the Polar Parlor was located in quite a tourist hot stop – situated perfectly between the main waterfall attractions and the nightlife – the alleyway of the Parlor's back entrance was currently completely obscured by Sergey's large cargo truck.

"Things good with shop, yes? Business okay?" Sergey asked as he fiddled with several heavy locks on the cargo door.

Elli smiled, twirling a strand of golden hair. "It's booming, sugar."

The door of the truck lifted up, releasing a puff of refrigerated air. Sergey stepped aside, letting Elli climb up the hatch.

She ran through a quick mental roster as she scanned the shipment. Ice cream tubs of a few sizes and many flavor varieties lined the truck shelves, while the floor was stacked with boxes and crates labeled *Polar Parlor Frozen Desserts; Trademark of Niagara Co.*

She hummed, running a manicured fingertip along the branded ice cream labels. "Winter Mint, Chocolate Falls, Klondike Crumble..."

Elli picked up a tub of Caribou Tracks ice cream – a Polar Parlor specialty – positioned underneath the other flavors. It rattled in response as she popped open the cover, exposing a collection of steel and metal pieces.

She inspected the parts, ensuring their sturdiness and quality. Magazines, receivers, bolts and pistons. Barrels. Her eyes twinkled with the delight of a little girl receiving a Lego set for Christmas. Precious firearms, some assembly required.

"Will you help me bring these in just over yonder,

Serge?" Elli nudged one of the sturdy wooden crates with her shoe. "I can take the ice cream, but these are much too heavy for me alone. I'll give ya a moving bonus."

Sergey eagerly scampered up the cargo hold with a quick nod, "Always a pleasure doing business, Ms. Elli."

A couple of miles away, just behind the employee entrance of the Bella Luna Winery in Niagara's touristy Little Italy district, two men were helping the ice wine truck driver unload his cargo.

It had taken all three of them the better part of an hour, as one of the men in a Bella Luna Winery t-shirt had insisted on counting and re-counting the shipment – for accuracy.

"Here's the last of it, Nicky." The driver said, rolling over a final barrel of wine towards the other man. "Got your numbers all aligned?"

"Look man, it's about the brand. Attention to detail, commitment to quality, right?" Nick stopped the barrel with his hands, standing it upright and gingerly prying it open.

Liquid sloshed within, and the sweet, fruity smell of ice wine wafted out as Nick stuck his arm inside and pulled out a casing containing various types of bullets. This particular barrel of Vidal Blanc hid 7.5mm hollow point bullets, and some incendiary rounds as a favor to the Don.

The driver got back into the truck, starting it up. "Hey, one more thing before I forget. There's some new bozo at the Rainbow Bridge toll gate."

The second man in a Bella Luna shirt, with a crooked nametag reading *Mike L.* peered up from his task of stacking barrels of wine on top of each other. "A new border guy? Did he make you go around?"

"Nah, but he did seem antsy about the deal. Might want to get Don Nové on it, in case he causes trouble."

Nick and Mike exchanged glances.

"Right," Nick said after a short pause. "We'll do that."

That evening, five people gathered in a rustic office on the floor above the Polar Parlor. Its windows overlooked the Niagara River border, seamlessly dividing Canada and the United States by the Hell's Half Acre and the roaring falls.

The office had a large wooden desk that stood along the window. Across from the desk sat Elli, no longer in her Polar Parlor apron, along with Mike and Nick, no longer in their Bella Luna shirts.

Elli had one leg crossed over the other and was casually skimming some texts on her phone. To an outsider, the blonde may catch your attention with her extraverted personality or perhaps her striking figure, but most would write her off as a sweet Southern sorority girl. This would be a mistake.

Elli was known better underground as The Businessman.

Next to her sat Nick, leaning back in his chair. He had changed into a white suit, emphasizing his dark hair and aging his face, which showed a history of conflict through a tapestry of scars. A Sicilian from the West Coast, he brought with him all the knowledge of *La Cosa Nostra* that he left behind following a deep betrayal. He was known as The Negotiator.

Closest to the desk, was Mike. Younger than Nick but

older than Elli, Mike was a lightweight young man in his late 20s, maybe early 30s, with a big nose and big brown eyes. Among the five people in the room, he was perhaps the most average. Which is why no one knew how he came to be known as the Boss's Bodyguard.

There was also a woman that stood in the corner of the room, a new recruit named Lucy. She rarely spoke since joining, and the other three didn't know much about her. Just that she was exceedingly quiet, exceptionally strong, and that her title was The Mercenary.

Fifth was the man seated behind the desk. He cleared his throat, folded up a newspaper, and gazed at each of the attendees with piercing blue eyes.

"Good evening, team. What've you got to report?"

Sebastian Nové. The Boss of the Niagara Co.

THREE
CUBES

- Toronto. September 2, 2013 -

The 18th floor boardroom was cold and featureless. Aside from a clock and a few framed posters of vague, bilingual company mantras, nothing held Noa's attention for long. Instead, he studied his interviewers.

The French-Canadian woman, Agent Lavoie, was preoccupied with her laptop. She seemed utterly disinterested in Noa. In fact, she made her indifference clearly visible on her face as she clacked angrily on the keys.

Noa thought she bore some resemblance to his old headmistress, Sister Ingrid, from whom he used to pick-pocket loose change and the occasional cigarette. Lavoie had a similar grimace, and given the opportunity, Noa figured she would be quite the similar disciplinarian.

Her composed colleague, Agent Koven, took a seat beside her, diagonally from Noa. He had a cool demeanor and a dignified air about him, but the faded dark circles hugging his eyes betrayed long hours of work invested in maintaining this front.

The agent had a piece of paper in front of him, on which Noa could make out the upside-down barebones description of himself:

Noa Sinclair
D.O.B. November 11, 1997
St. Isidore's Collegiate – Graduate of 2013
Specialization: Computer Science & Programming

Below that were bullet-point summaries of projects he'd accomplished abroad, some volunteer work, some minor inventions.

He doubted they read any of it.

"So, Noa." Agent Koven smiled at him again. "First off, welcome to Canada. Is it your first time here?"

Noa considered his friendliness with skepticism. They had already started the interview late, and were going to proceed with small talk? He wasn't very good at small talk. In fact, he wasn't a big fan of talking in general.

But Noa needed roughly five minutes and a two-meter range of at least one of the agents' laptops while it was connected to the corporate VPN, and he needed to stall for time.

So, he nodded politely and returned the smile. "Yes. It's very... vast."

"That it is," Koven said with a half-laugh. "Nothing like where you're from, I bet. St. Isidore's, right? Impressive reputation. I understand that they set up young, er, *professionals* such as yourself with internships around the world."

From behind her computer screen, Agent Lavoie barely contained a scoff.

"What interested you in CSIS, Noa?" Koven asked.

With his right hand, Noa repositioned his glasses in

mock thoughtfulness. His other, pocketed hand grasped the little cubed device engraved with an 11. He ran his thumb around the edges.

What indeed?

Father Emilio, headmaster of St. Isidore's Home for Extraordinary Children, made it very clear in his parting words to Noa that failure was not an option. He would have one chance to secure this placement. The Home's credibility was never enough to sway a hiring manager's opinions.

The kids of St. Isidore's had to be ready for creative means of persuasion, lest they be banished to the streets of whichever country they traveled to without a return ticket.

Noa glanced out the window. Lake Ontario peeked out through a myriad of glass and concrete structures.

"The border."

"The border?" Agent Koven echoed. "Can you elaborate? I'm assuming you mean the US-Canadian border. What about it?"

Noa withheld a sigh. "I *could* tell you what interests me about it. I could tell you how I find it fascinating – the way the pieces fit together like a well-oiled game of Tetris along the evergreen perimeter and over the shipwrecks of the great lakes – the flawless exchange of drugs and firearms and god knows else. But I know you don't really care."

"Pardon me?" Koven asked, his voice betraying some shock.

"Are you really considering my employment?"

Koven hesitated, but Agent Lavoie at last looked up from her computer.

"No," she stated matter-of-factly. "We were told to entertain this quote, unquote interview, but seriously, did they think we would hire a child? Outrageous."

"Miriam," Koven started, but she went on.

"No, Alex, the world is harsh, and Noam should know it."

Noa glanced at the clock on the wall. "It's Noa, actually. You know, like the ark."

She peered at the paper in front of her partner. "Noa-*h*?"

"There's no 'h'," he said. "It's not a typo."

"Don't take a tone with me, young man." Lavoie sat up straighter, and Noa felt validated in his earlier comparison. She lectured just like a Catholic headmistress. "We took time out of our busy days to meet with you, because of your school's international renown. You came here on an all-expense paid flight, expecting to get a job on a silver platter?"

Koven sighed into his hands. "This isn't going well."

On the contrary, thought Noa, five excruciatingly long minutes had almost passed.

"For my own curiosity," Noa said, tearing his eyes away from the clock on the wall and facing Agent Lavoie. "What kind of applicant *are* you looking for?"

"Older, at the very least," she replied. "Five, ten more years and maybe I would consider you. A university education, experience in your field, just as a start. You can go back and tell your teachers that experience in Canadian intelligence and law enforcement would help next time."

Noa knew there would not be a next time. St. Isidore only houses children until their graduation placement has been assigned. CSIS was his assignment.

Agent Koven spoke up, with a much softer voice. "That's not to say you can't offer us bright ideas. We need young people to help pave the way for change, especially in the digital landscape—"

"Look, Norman." Lavoie peered at him over her spectacles. "My colleague is just being polite. The cases we work are unbelievably complex, and we simply do not have the time to train every 'young person' that comes our way. Maybe one day you'll understand."

"It's Noa. Like the ark." He looked at the clock again. Finally. "I suppose I might as well take my leave then. Thank you for your time."

Noa stood and held out his right hand awkwardly. The sleeve of the oversized suit jacket had rolled down again, hiding most of his hand, and making him look even smaller.

Koven stood as well, while Lavoie remained seated.

"I hope our paths will cross again soon," said Koven. He shook Noa's hand once.

Noa smiled, his left hand still hidden his pocket. "Me too, Agent Koven."

Once the boardroom door had closed, Lavoie flung her head back in the chair. "God! What a waste of time."

"He seemed like a bright kid, Miriam." Koven stood by the door, ensuring it was closed. "You didn't need to be so cold."

"No, you need to toughen up, Alex," she said and spun her laptop around to face him. "How much time were you planning on wasting? This meeting invite came through 10 minutes ago. You and I are both supposed to present to the Director at 11:00."

"What? That's in less than an hour," Koven stammered, pulling his work phone out of his pocket and scrolling through emails. "Shit."

"Yeah. Sounds like the Director wants an update on the

insider trading activity in the South and on your new cyber security team. We're really lagging behind our Q2 targets, mostly because of that Great Lakes syndicate. Oh, maybe you'll join me on the Niagara case? If your team is ready."

"That could be a huge break," Koven nodded. "I need to prep Lee and Sanders. We won't get on an agenda like this again for weeks."

"*Bon*, you're welcome," Lavoie said, shutting her laptop and packing it away. "If I hadn't sent that boy on his way, you wouldn't have time to prepare at all."

"You can at least try to remember his name, Miriam." Koven turned to open the door, and hesitated. "Come to think of it, did we ever introduce ourselves to him?"

As the agents shrugged off this thought with some uncertainty, Noa had already returned to the safety of the bathroom stall. He plugged in the little cube from his pocket into his laptop and waited for the 11 insignia to light up.

His stomach grumbled.

Balancing a myriad of electronics on his lap, Noa fumbled with his backpack and found the half-eaten donut from the morning's scouting mission. He stuffed it in his mouth and started up a familiar game on his phone while the computer loaded.

---

11 o'clock.

Director Colson's office faced the harbor. The view of the lake was spectacular, but the reflection of the sun created a slight glare on the presentation monitor, which was currently displaying the meeting agenda.

Junior Agents Lee and Sanders had entered first, exchanging nervous pleasantries with their boss's superior.

They were followed shortly by Agent Lavoie and Agent Koven.

"Good morning," the director began. "I'm glad we could make this work on such short notice. Miriam, I've been very impressed by the caliber of your work in the last quarter, so I wanted to get an update on your next steps. Alex, I'm looking forward to hearing about your cyber team launch as well."

Lavoie and Koven glanced at each other briefly with some confusion.

"Thank you, ma'am," Lavoie cleared her throat. "I have the latest financial surveillance for the quarter and the report on the Great Lakes syndicate activity, but, if I could just clarify, which achievements are you referring to?"

Director Colson looked at her strangely. "Now, hold on, I thought you booked this time to discuss the St. Lawrence and Rideau mafia trades. Your analyst sent me those reports this morning, they were phenomenal."

"What reports? Which analyst?" Lavoie fought to keep her composure as she scanned dozens of emails in her inbox.

Agent Lee, a timid software developer and junior agent in the cybercrime division, leaned over to his boss. "Didn't the Director book this meeting?"

Koven nodded. He had thought so too.

Director Colson connected a cable to her computer, projecting a meticulously crafted report on the large office display. The summary was organized by time and region, detailing a series of events that pieced together the financial dealings of two criminal organizations.

"This is..." Lavoie stared. "This project went on hold two months ago, ma'am. We knew Rideau had connections to Bay Street and had been trading with the St. Lawrence

Gang, but the fund and asset movements were untraceable. This was an unfinished operation."

The director flipped through the slides. "That's not what it looks like, Miriam. Maybe your analyst finished it for you in secret," she chuckled. "Either way, whoever completed this, it's worthy of a commendation. I'll send this through to execution, unless you've got anything to add?"

Lavoie struggled to hide the lines of concern gathering on her forehead. "Could you forward this to me? I must have misplaced it."

"Sure, sure," the director shrugged as she unplugged her computer from the display. "Alright, how about we hear from you then, Alex? Will you demonstrate what the digital budget has been funding for the past few months?"

"Yes ma'am," Koven motioned to the two junior agents. "You've met Agent Sanders; he's leading the risk and regulation initiative and translating it to the virtual world. And Agent Lee joins us from MIT and heading up software development and programming."

"Great," said Colson, "show me what you've developed."

Lee took the time during Koven's introduction to connect his computer to the giant screen. It now displayed a mock-up version of the CSIS website, featuring the cybersecurity landing page.

"This version of our site isn't live to the public yet, but we've added new resources for users to access." Koven said, nodding at Lee. The younger agent clicked through the intranet.

Koven continued, "Over the past few weeks, we've been beta-testing a new bot that can detect fraudulent activity by leveraging fraud alerts from bank accounts, and we're hoping—"

Agent Lavoie stood suddenly, her chair banging against the office wall behind her with an impact.

"Miriam?" Director Colson and everyone else turned to look at her. "You okay?"

"Apologies, ma'am," Lavoie managed, collecting her things from the table. "I need to speak to Agent Koven outside. Urgently. Now. Sorry." She slammed her computer shut and hurried out of the director's office.

Koven stood, glancing at the door and then at the director. "I, uh, should probably see what's going on. I'm terribly sorry about this. Lee, please take over for me – show Director Colson the new pages on the intranet site. I'll be right back!"

With a nod from the director, Koven chased after the other agent, who was waiting for him in the hallway. Her arms were crossed, and her brows were furrowed.

"What the hell, Miriam?"

"Come with me," she said, leading him to the nearest stairwell. Once inside, she looked around frantically for any people on the flights above or below them.

"This is ridiculous," said Koven. "What's going on? I left my subordinates in there with Colson, they're going to be traumatized. I need to get back."

"Alex. Listen," Lavoie lowered her voice, looking him in the eyes. "I don't have any analysts working for me."

Koven frowned. "Right. I thought not."

"Colson forwarded me the email she got from my supposed analyst this morning. It doesn't have a signature or anything, it just says 'from Agent Lavoie's analyst.' And the data, Alex, it's insane. We've been trying to access those records for years. Overseas accounts, shell logging companies in Montreal, hard evidence of insider trading through Internet Relays."

"That doesn't make sense," said Koven. "What email did it come from?"

"That's the thing!" Lavoie's hushed voice had gradually become a hushed shouting. "It came from *my* email, Alex!"

"Shit," Koven grimaced. "That is worrying. You're sure it's not just someone on your team that cracked this case without your knowledge?"

"We tried every route, it was impossible. The project was closed! You couldn't even access the Rideau-Lawrence file directory without my password." Lavoie was pacing now.

Koven reached for his phone. "I think Lee can help with this. Maybe we can trace that email – oh, no. Sanders called. Twice. I need to get back to the director's meeting."

"What a nightmare of a day," Lavoie muttered, following the other agent back down the hall to the south-side corner office.

The two agents let themselves back inside, hoping they did not look as flustered as they felt. They were greeted with the pale faces of agents Lee and Sanders, and a very amused Director Colson.

"Glad you could join us again, Alex!" The director said with a smile that worried Agent Koven greatly. "These two were just showing me the interactive game you built into the new site. I can't say it's quite my taste, but I appreciate the creativity."

"I beg your pardon?" Koven turned to face the screen, which was still displaying the mock-up website on the CSIS intranet. His eyes went wide.

Starting from the Government of Canada banner at the very top, various assortments of brightly colored square blocks were raining down over the text on the page. A few of the pieces were starting to accumulate at the bottom of the page, right over the paragraph about cyber-attacks.

Sanders inched over to his boss. "When we tried to exit, the system wouldn't respond. Even the task manager isn't working," he whispered. "So, the director said she wanted to see it through. She thinks you did this."

Koven struggled to breathe evenly. "This is Tetris. It's a game of *Tetris*."

"You should have added the Russian music, Alex!" Director Colson laughed. "Oh, what's this now?"

Alongside the stacking and disappearing cubes, a leaderboard appeared. The more blocks vanished from the screen, the higher the score grew.

"This is really something else. Who's playing? Or is it pre-programmed? Will you let the website users play?" Director Colson asked. "Not that I'm condoning this usage of your time and my budget."

The leaderboard hit 1,000,000 points and stopped counting. The colorful square pieces stopped descending from the top of the site page.

"It's over?" Lee gasped, gripping Sanders' elbow.

Instead of blocks, the screen started filling up with pixelated water. It flooded in from all sides and rose to about halfway, until it reached the leaderboard.

The leaderboard then displayed ALEX KOVEN & MIRIAM LAVOIE in big block letters.

Director Colson looked at the two agents. "Miriam, you're in on this? And what's with the sudden flood?"

Koven and Lavoie were speechless.

From the left side of the webpage, a little boat floated atop the water and sailed over to the center of the screen. There was a humanoid figure on it and a handful of animals.

"Oh, how cute," said Colson. "Noah's Ark, right?"

The room was silent for a moment.

Agent Lavoie sank into a chair. "*Merde.*"

St. Isidore's Home is partially an orphanage, partially scholastic, strictly religious, and entirely shrouded in secrecy.

Located in the Principality of Monaco, St. Isidore's sits atop a steep cliff, overlooking the Mediterranean coastline. The Home itself has an imposing structure, with a historic chapel attached to the main building, a massive iron gate, and tall brick walls embracing it on all sides.

Inside St. Isidore's walls, just before the orphanage itself, stands a fountain with a square, elegantly decorated with bushes and flowers. They are almost always abuzz with bees.

The Home is said to produce exceptionally brilliant members of society. Its graduates can be found worldwide, working in various specialties. Medical research, Fortune 500, tech innovation, international intelligence agencies. A St. Isidore graduate must be fluent in many languages, outstanding in their field, and strive for the betterment of society, upholding the Home's reputation.

Not much else is known about St. Isidore's, except that its training tactics are severe, and that only a handful of specially-selected children are accommodated at any given time.

Perfer et obdura, dolor hic tibi proderit olim. Be patient and tough; someday this pain will be useful to you. The Headmaster's favorite Roman proverb. It is ingrained in the young orphans' minds; repeated ad nauseam by the teachers and caretakers alike. Their fancy, Catholic way of saying "no pain, no gain."

The children would come from all ends of the globe, scouted by either the headmasters of the Home or recommended by word of mouth to the right network of people. Upon arrival, the child would be stripped of their name and given the name of a month to go by instead. And just as there are only 12 months in a calendar year, there are only ever 12 attendees at a time.

Once they graduate, usually at the age of 18, the children could reinstate their name if they remember it. Sometimes they just picked a new one.

In summer of 2013, St. Isidore's 15th Generation November was notified that he was eligible for an early graduation. Father Emilio had called the boy into his office, given him a one-way plane ticket and his assignment, and repeated the St. Isidore motto one last time: *Perfer et obdura...*

Has my Dolor *finally paid off?* The 15th Generation November waited impatiently in the lobby of the CSIS building. About half an hour had passed since the agents had their meeting. He nervously plucked at the hem of his sweater sleeve, having dumped the suit jacket as soon as he left the 18th floor.

I may have gone too far, he thought with a frown, gazing down at his frayed shoes. If he did not succeed in getting this position, how was he expected to survive in this strange city on his own? Or worse – *What if they think I'm some sort of terrorist? What if they detain me?*

Such harrowing thoughts were interrupted when his field of vision became obstructed by a pair of beige high-heeled shoes.

"Noa Sinclair, I presume?"

St. Isidore's 15th Generation November, now known as Noa, found that his throat suddenly became very dry. This was not the voice of either agent Koven or Lavoie, and it did not sound very friendly.

He glanced up to meet the gaze of the voice's owner, but had immense trouble maintaining eye contact. He recognized her immediately from the CSIS archives. With bated breath, Noa nodded.

"Certainly not what I was expecting," said Director Colson, keeping her voice quiet but firm. "I understand from your profile that you are a child, however your actions demonstrate a considerable level of intellect and boldness, dare I say *audacity*, so I will speak to you as an adult. *Stand.*"

Noa stood immediately, color draining from his face. He had to crane his neck up as the director hovered at least half a foot taller.

"Noa Sinclair," the director began, "do you understand that accessing private data and hijacking our intranet servers is a severe and punishable offense in this country? And that your little game with my agents, while cheeky, is crude and illegal?"

Noa tried to suppress the overwhelming urge to run or, perhaps, to vomit. "Ma'am," he said in an almost inaudible mumble, "I have no idea what you're talking about."

Director Colson leaned in a little closer, studying the boy's face. He drew back.

"Your reaction tells a different story, kid." The director said.

Noa tried to remember the script he prepared for this situation but wavered under the director's bone-chilling stare. The intensity of her presence was overwhelming, and he felt as if he were becoming smaller the longer she glared at him.

He hesitated a moment, then took off his glasses.

The sharp-angled director now a blur of messy lines in his vision, Noa sucked in a breath and stood a little straighter. He narrowed his focus on his words and the sensation of the frames in his hands.

"I suppose," he said softly, "if what you're saying is true, then it's quite dangerous that your systems are so exposed and that your data can be so easily accessed by an outsider." The noise of the lobby faded around them as he anchored himself firmly onto the ground. "If what you're saying is true, then perhaps this individual could assist in not only strengthening your existing security, but also ensuring such a hack does not occur again."

His voice became a bit more confident as he continued. "If, again, what you're saying is true. However, the burden of proving it would surely be difficult, as I'm certain this individual would not leave a trace to their identity."

The director stared down at him. "You've got guts kid; I'll give you that."

Noa put his glasses back on, after an unconvincing display of cleaning them on his sweater. "I'm sure I don't know what you mean, ma'am."

Director Colson massaged the crease of her brows. "Alright, Sinclair. So, in your unbiased opinion, if I allow this 'individual' onto my team, he would reveal how he got the inaccessible information and penetrated our security systems? That's quite beneficial to us."

"I would imagine so, yes," Noa answered quickly.

"And why wouldn't we simply detain this individual upon hearing his confession, and have him tell us by force?"

"Because," Noa said with the slightest hint of a smile,

"there is a chance this individual might have foreseen such an outcome and might release such a humiliating incident to the public upon being apprehended. But he might consider *not* doing so in exchange for a job and guaranteed immunity."

A brief silence lingered between them.

Some government employees passing through the lobby would look at this interaction and wonder why the Director of the Canadian Security Intelligence Service was speaking to a teenager, but no one dared to interrupt.

The director shook her head with a quiet laugh. "No wonder I couldn't get any intel on Isidore interns from my friends in the states or MI6. You little rugrats get them in a chokehold, and the world just thinks it's an easy job placement. Clever."

Noa just smiled.

"Okay, kid." She extended her hand, "Probation period. 6 months. If you can play nice with Alex and Miriam, consider yourself an agent-in-training."

Noa practically heaved a sigh of relief. He shook her hand, "Thank you, ma'am!"

FOUR
STAINED GLASS

- Venice, Italy. February 7, 2014 -

"What's this thing, Boss? Orange juice?"

"Spritz. Venetian specialty."

The *Caffè Centrale* in St. Mark's Square was bustling with tourists despite the season.

Ignoring all the other patrons, a number of waiters were busy attending to two men seated at a single table by the window. They hung on every word of the one on the right, who had picked up a chilled cocktail and took a single, tantalizingly slow sip.

"How is it, Boss?" said the one on the left, studying the orange drink.

The wait staff trembled in anticipation.

The man on the right, Sebastian Nové, placed the glass down. The ice clinked inside. "It's alright." He turned to the waiters. *"La prossima volta, usa un prosecco di qualità superiore."*

"Si, signore!" The waiters quickly scattered, one of them hitting another upside the head.

"So, no tip then?" The man across from Sebastian said, taking a sip of the drink himself. "Hey, it's not that bad."

"No tipping in Europe, Mike." Sebastian glanced at his watch. "You can have mine, if you like it. We need to leave soon."

"Will do," Mike took another swig of the Spritz. "Boss, not that I mind the sightseein' and all, but if we're meeting up with your guy this late, why'd we fly in yesterday?"

Sebastian felt an unseen, comforting presence tightly folded up inside the hidden pocket above his heart. "Nothing for you to be concerned with, Mike. I just needed to test something."

"You got it, Boss. No questions asked."

Once Mike had finished both cocktails, the two men left the café in St. Mark's Square and made their way through the canals, bridges and cobblestoned side streets of Venice towards the lagoon. Desperate for customers during the slow winter season, street vendors and gondoliers endlessly tried to get their attention.

The two of them looked more like lawyers or investment bankers on an international business trip than tourists, with their expensive suits and overcoats, but Mike still fell for a few traps, stopping to look at knick-knacks and try Italian treats.

Sebastian paid no attention to the street vendors or any pedestrians for the matter, and most scurried out of his way.

Once they reached the edge of the Venetian mainland, Sebastian approached the No. 9 Vaporetto stop. Mike had caught up, after getting left behind a couple times along the way.

"We're takin' a ferry somewhere, Boss?" he asked, looking out to the lagoon. Despite the chilled air, the emerald waters were calm and less crowded than usual.

Sebastian had just finished saying something in Italian to the boat's captain when Mike joined him on the dock. "Yes, not far. Small island just North of Venice."

He gave a nod to the ferryman as the two of them boarded the waterbus.

The ferryman quickly cordoned off the queue, muttering apologies in English and Italian to the tourists gathering at the harbor.

"I didn't know you had such a reputation here!" Mike said, impressed.

As the waterbus departed from the marina, Sebastian took a seat at the nose of the boat.

"Before the Niagara Co., I had a lot of business here." He gazed out onto the green water.

Mike joined him, following his gaze with unease. "...Do you miss it?"

Sebastian inhaled the cool winter breeze. "I suppose part of me does. It's a beautiful city. Not a stain in the sapphire sky, not a ripple on the palace-walled canals." Then he grimaced, "I don't miss the stink, though. And the trades were inefficient."

Mike chuckled, "It does smell a bit like a port-a-potty sometimes."

They sat in comfortable silence for the rest of the short boat ride. In about ten minutes, the vaporetto pulled up to a ferry terminal and slowed to a stop. The sign above read *Murano Colonna*.

"This is our stop," Sebastian said as he exited the vaporetto, handing the ferryman an envelope with a quiet *grazie*.

Mike hopped off. "Murano, huh. Never heard of it."

Sebastian made his way through the small town of Murano, followed closely by Mike. The streets were mostly empty as evening approached, and the chill in the air tightened its wintery grip.

They walked briskly alongside a narrow canal and then crossed two bridges until they were in a desolate square on the Northeastern side of the tiny island. Sebastian stopped in front of an occupied bench that faced the canal.

"I expected a more scenic location from you, Rocco. This is a bit," he gestured to the decaying buildings around them, "*deprimente.*"

The man on the bench gave an exaggerated shrug. "I thought you would appreciate my humor, *Signore Nové.*"

"Ah, yes," Sebastian turned to look down the brick-paved path from which they came, street sign illuminated dully by a single lamp. "*Campiello de le Case Nové.* On the *Fondamenta de le Case Nové.*"

"Even though you don't own Murano, it certainly seems like you do," said Rocco. "Why don't you have a seat with me? I'm grateful that you came all this way."

"If you insist." Sebastian took a seat, as Mike took up his post at his boss's side. "It's getting dark, though."

"This won't take long." Rocco smiled insincerely.

Rocco Maniero. A plump *Mala del Brenta* Venetian mobster with a round face and beady eyes. Sebastian had a hunch as to the purpose behind his invitation but wanted to confirm. Before he could though, the ringing of Mike's cellphone interrupted his thoughts.

"Sorry, sorry! That's me." Mike answered it, "Hello? Oh, hey El', what's up?"

Rocco eyed Mike incredulously. Sebastian just waited.

"Huh. I'm not sure, let me ask him," Mike lowered the phone a bit and leaned down to Sebastian. "Boss, Elli says there's some high school kid askin' for a part-time job at the Parlor."

Sebastian sighed, "The shop front is hers to do with as she pleases."

Mike nodded, "You heard him, Elli! Looks like you're the boss now. I've gotta run though, we're kind of in the middle of something here. Later." He slid the phone back into his pocket.

"Apologies," Sebastian looked back to Rocco Maniero like nothing happened. "How've you been, Rocco? How's the family? Lucia and the kids?"

The other man's smile faded. "They are well. And you? Still living the young, bachelor life in the land of the free?"

"I've always preferred the company of myself and my work," Sebastian replied. "Speaking of which, I trust business is going well? Or is that the reason behind our impromptu meet-up?"

Sebastian noticed the lines on Rocco's forehead tighten slightly.

"Before we get to that, I wanted to show you something." Rocco opened his briefcase as Mike instinctively reached for his gun. "Tell your crony to relax, would you? I'm unarmed here."

Sebastian knew that was a lie, but waved Mike down. He watched attentively as Rocco removed a small object covered in paper and carefully unwrapped it.

"Remember this?" Rocco tossed the wrapping onto the ground and held out a delicate, hand-blown crystalline figurine of a translucent sky-blue dove. "Quality Murano glass, unlike any other."

Sebastian took the statuette and examined it gingerly in the lamplight. "Attention to detail; commitment to quality."

Mike leaned over to look at it too. The little glass bird, mostly transparent, reflected hues of blue and speckles of white in the glow of the lamp above them.

"Our first one," said Rocco. "I kept it. Call me sentimental."

Sebastian cradled the glass dove in his hand affectionately. "Amateur work compared to the ones in the market now. How many grams does our feathered friend carry? One hundred?"

"Still, there's something to be said about your first," Rocco took the bird back. "I kept the first opium infused butterfly too, you know."

Sebastian leaned against the back of the bench. "This reminiscence is nice Rocco, but I imagine you'll be getting to the point soon. Has there been a drug bust? Trouble with the mainland trade? Supplier negotiations?"

Rocco's chubby fingers squeezed the crystal figurine. "No, nothing like that, Nové. Quite the opposite actually. I'm proposing to expand the business."

"Oh?"

"In fact," Rocco continued, "I'd like to take it off your hands."

Sebastian was intrigued. "I must say, I anticipated a multitude of potential responses, Rocco, but this was not one of them. Are you offering to buy out my stake in the Mala del Brenta?"

The mobster looked over at him with some agitation. "Why is that a surprise? Word on the street is that the old Nové is gone – lost interest in the coca and the poppy – and sits back comfortably gambling on stocks these days instead."

"And your proposal is what, exactly?" Sebastian asked. "That I should leave the trafficking to you and the Mala del Brenta, and stick to insider trading?"

"You wouldn't have gotten your start here without me

and my *zio*, Nové." Rocco said in a warning tone. "It would be fair for you, really. I would give you a cut of the profits in perpetuity."

Sebastian let out a sharp laugh. Rocco, startled, nearly dropped the bird figurine from his lap.

"Rocco, you delight me. Your *zio*? 'Angel Face' Maniero?" He composed himself, straightening out his suit. "Your scheme is becoming clear to me now."

"What are you going on about, Nové?" Rocco demanded.

Sebastian ignored him and leaned his head back to look at Mike. "Have you heard of his uncle, Mike? 'Angel Face' Maniero. Biggest name in the Venetian mafia. Well, used to be."

Mike shook his head. "No, Boss. What about him?"

"As of today, from what I know, he turned out to be a *pentito*." Sebastian emphasized each syllable, making direct eye contact with Rocco while doing so. "Which means our friend here has been disingenuous with us about the state of affairs in the city of marble walls and sunken halls."

"Pen-ti-toe?" Mike repeated, "What's that?"

Rocco had stood at this point, face red and nostrils flaring. "How could you possibly know that?"

"A *pentito* is a narc, Mike. His *zio* squealed to the law, which means the backing of the Mala del Brenta has fallen through, isn't that right?" Sebastian said unemotionally, watching Rocco's movements like a hawk.

"That's impossible. He just went to them today," Rocco managed to say, "the plan was family-only; who told you? How did you figure it out?"

Sebastian stood as well. "I'm more curious about your so-called business proposal, Rocco. Let's say I didn't know about your cowardly deception and went along with your story. What's next?"

Rocco clenched the fist that wasn't holding the figurine. "An investment," he grumbled.

"Pardon me?"

"An investment," he spat. "I would have asked you for an investment into our— that is, my new business. I know you have a stash of millions of euros hidden somewhere in Murano. Everyone in del Brenta knows that. I would have asked you to take me there."

"Aha," Sebastian noted the slight movement of Rocco's right hand and shot a quick glance at Mike. "And if I had refused to show you?"

"I wouldn't have let you refuse." Rocco dropped the crystalline dove and reached into his coat, drawing a pistol. As the poor bird shattered to fragments of glass on the brick, two weapons were simultaneously revealed.

Rocco held aim at Sebastian's chest. Mike had a gun pointed at Rocco's head.

"This was your grand plan?" Sebastian frowned. "I'm disappointed."

"Sometimes the simplest way is the best way," said Rocco. "You millennials with your innovations think you're hot shit, but you're not so hot staring death in the face."

"It would seem we are at a stalemate." Sebastian gestured to the guns around them.

Rocco grinned, gold crowns glinting in the lamplight. "You *will* tell me where you hid that cash, Nové." His eyes moved to rest on Mike's forehead.

Mike didn't move. "Sniper, Boss?"

Sebastian sighed. "How dull. And of course, once I showed you where the money is hidden, you'd have killed me anyway?"

Rocco's grin stayed plastered on his face, "Think of it this way, Nové! Venezia is a beautiful grave."

"You've got a point there, old friend," Sebastian hummed. "Still, I'm not quite ready to die yet. For the days are not full enough, and the nights are not full enough, and life slips by like a field mouse not shaking the grass."

"Stalling won't work," said Rocco. "Take me to the spot now, or I tell my man to shoot."

Sebastian looked over at Mike, who was starting to break out in a sweat. "Why don't you give it a try?"

"What? Are you serious?" Rocco sputtered. "Your men mean so little to you?"

Mike's terrified expression vanished almost instantly and was replaced by an awe-struck stare. Rocco worryingly followed that stare up to his own forehead.

"You—! But how?" Rocco searched either of them for a sign of the sniper sight's red dot, but unable to find it, reached the worst possible conclusion. "You set me up! *Bastardo!*"

"You can't be upset, *Amico*. You did it first," Sebastian shrugged.

"Wait!" Rocco begged, "Tell me, how did you—"

A single, silent shot pierced through the evening air.

Rocco Maniero's body swayed unsteadily for a few seconds, then toppled over, into the green canal with a forceful splash.

Wiping away the droplets with a gloved hand, Sebastian knelt down by the shards of the broken dove. "I would have liked to keep this. What a pity."

Mike put his gun away and sat on the bench, heaving out a long breath. "That was a close call, Boss! You should be more worried about yourself than that little statue."

"We were never in any danger," Sebastian said, getting up. "Well, I suppose there was a slight margin of error."

"What do you mean, Boss? Did you know this would happen?"

As Mike posed the question, a third person in a dark cloak joined them in the square. She took off her hood.

"Lucy?" Mike gaped at her, "When did you get to Italy?"

Lucy didn't answer. She merely gave a curt nod to her boss.

"Well done," he said. "You left the body and sign?"

She nodded again.

"Great," Sebastian swept the remnants of the shattered figurine into the canal. "Then let us take our leave."

Mike continued to stare at Lucy as they walked back to the Murano harbor. "I'm so confused, Boss! Why didn't Lucy just fly with us?"

"I told you Mike, I had to test something. That meant maintaining stable variables and keeping you in the dark," Sebastian said as they approached their private vaporetto.

This time, there was no ferryman. Lucy took the helm and started up the boat.

"Are we taking a different route back to Venice?" Mike asked, sitting down in front with Sebastian.

"Yes. We'll be making a stop at San Michele, near Murano."

Mike caught on. "That's where you hid the money. Ha! He really thought you'd tell him."

Sebastian smiled. "I did tell him, actually."

The vaporetto pushed off from the dock, albeit not as smoothly as before.

"You did?"

"San Michele is a cemetery island. The money is hidden in a tomb," Sebastian said.

"You never told him that. Did you?" Mike wondered.

"*And the days are not full enough, and the nights are not full enough.*" Sebastian quoted again. "Ezra Pound. May he rest in peace on San Michele, along with my 17.8 million euros."

FIVE

THE CALL

- Toronto. February 7, 2014 -

Just before eight in the morning, Noa powered on his computer. He watched the sun creep over the horizon, rising slowly over the frigid waters of Lake Ontario. One of the very, very few benefits offered by Noa's new office, especially in winter.

A DOS-type screen loaded at last and Noa placed his coffee mug down with some reluctance.

```
[WELCOME TO THE CANADIAN SECURITY INTELLI-
GENCE DIRECT ACCESS TERMINAL. PLEASE ENTER
YOUR LOGIN AND USER AUTHENTICATION]
> sa_n_sinclair@csis.net | n0vemb3r15
[LOGIN CONFIRMED. PLEASE ENTER COMMAND.]
> access_file_GRT_LK_CLCTV
[WARNING! YOU ARE ATTEMPTING TO ACCESS A
SECURITY LEVEL 3 (CONFIDENTIAL) DIRECTORY.
ACCESS TO THIS DIRECTORY IS RESTRICTED TO
PERSONNEL WITH LEVEL 3 CLEARANCE. ACCESS
```

WITHOUT PROPER AUTHORIZATION WILL RESULT IN
DISCIPLINARY ACTION UP TO AND INCLUDING
TERMINATION. DO YOU WISH TO CONTINUE?]
> Y
[YOUR INFORMATION HAS BEEN LOGGED FOR
RECORD KEEPING AND INFORMATION SECURITY
PURPOSES. PLEASE RE-ENTER YOUR LOGIN AND
USER AUTHENTICATION NOW.]

Noa sighed. The authentication procedures had
become tedious after just a few days on the job, and half a
year later, they were downright annoying. Without looking
at the keys, he re-entered his login information.

> sa_n_sinclair@csis.net | n0vember15
[WARNING! INCORRECT AUTHENTICATION. YOU
HAVE SIXTY (60) SECONDS TO ENTER THE
CORRECT ACCESS INFORMATION OR SECURITY WILL
BE SUMMONED TO YOUR LOCATION.]

The sudden error tone from the computer caused Noa
to jerk in his seat. "Crap," he grumbled, "a typo?" He
hurriedly tapped the credentials again.

> sa_n_sinclair@csis.net | n0vember15
[WARNING! INCORRECT AUTHENTICATION. ONE (1)
ATTEMPT REMAINING.]

"Huh? Still wrong?" He panicked, squinting at the
screen. "Oh. 3, not e. Damn it."

> sa_n_sinclair@csis.net | n0vemb3r15

```
[AUTHENTICATION ACCEPTED. PLEASE ENTER YOUR
PROJECT-SPECIFIC PERSONAL IDENTIFICATION
NUMBER FOR FILE GRT_LK_CLCTV.]
> 332-705-NS
[PSPIN ACCEPTED. PLEASE LOOK INTO THE
CAMERA FOR A RETINAL IDENTIFICATION SCAN.]
```

Noa exhaled with relief, looking into the camera. He did not feel like dealing with security this early in the morning.

```
[INCORRECT ORIENTATION. PLEASE ALIGN THE
PUPILS OF YOUR EYES WITH THE GUIDELINES
INDICATED ON THE SECONDARY SCREEN AND TRY
AGAIN.]
```

Noa blinked. "Ugh, right." He quickly removed his glasses, placing them on the table near his mug.

```
[THANK YOU. THE TIME AND DATE OF YOUR
ACCESS TO THIS FILE DIRECTORY HAS BEEN
LOGGED AND REPORTED FOR RECORD KEEPING
PURPOSES.]
```
USER NAME: Special Agent Noa Sinclair
DIVISION: Cybercrime and Financial Crime Transnational Taskforce
DISPLAYING: GRT_LK_CLCTV | CLEARANCE LEVEL 3

"Finally," Noa rubbed his eyes and put his glasses back on. He reached for the coffee and took a sip. *Cold,* he thought with a pout.

Alone in the office this early in the morning, the

redhead continued the research on his team's case. Tired pine green eyes skimmed the pages on the monitor.

A collection of criminal syndicates, unofficially nicknamed the Great Lakes Collective due to their extensive reach from New York to Chicago and from Toronto to Thunder Bay above the border, had been gaining infamy for years.

The largest of the Great Lakes Collective, the Niagara Company, was thought to be the ringleader in the region. Although the trail of drug deals and arms trades always ran cold before it reached them. In fact, the Niagara Co. was unique in that they never bothered to hide their existence.

The group was known for being very particular about its branding. "Attention to detail, commitment to quality." This was the slogan for any Niagara Co. subsidiary, from wineries to publishing houses.

As the group's influence grew, pressure to track down the leader grew as well. The case concerned both US and Canadian officials, since this mafia operated flawlessly across the border at multiple crossing points. Agent Lavoie's team was already on the case by the time that Noa was hired at CSIS, and Agent Koven's team joined shortly thereafter.

Agents Koven and Lavoie, who were cautiously optimistic and vehemently opposed to his onboarding respectively, were building a case with the US authorities to track illicit activities on both sides of the border, mainly narcotics and firearms movement.

However, in summer of 2013, the situation changed.

Investment bankers, asset managers and financial advisors started receiving the Call.

Soon after, the online rumor mill picked up the buzz by trending *#thecall*. Journalists hung around Wall Street, interviewing brokers about their experience when they got *the Call*. Whether or not they actually got it, no one could confirm.

The fervor spread across the states, with news pundits spinning wild theories on the origin of the Call and the source of the mysterious voice behind it. Economists threatened a market collapse, but after a few months it became evident that the Calls were rare enough to sustain the game and profitable enough to capitalize on it.

Eventually, it seemed like the media attention was unwanted, and if people wanted to receive the elusive call, they had to shut up about it. But before the informational blackout, one stockbroker revealed the following:

In the summer of 2013, he received a call from an unknown ID. The voice introduced themselves as an anonymous financial consultant and said that if he wanted to get rich, he should follow the caller's investment advice. Then, the voice listed a couple stocks and a commodity, said they must be bought on the same day, and hung up.

The broker, torn between thinking it must be a prank but having heard the rumors, bought a hundred shares of just one of the stocks suggested by the anonymous caller that day.

To his amazement and delight, the share price jumped 50% overnight. The other stock and commodity named had grown as well. This was enough to solidify the enigma of the Call and spark an outrage across the world.

Was it real? A fabrication to cause mass hysteria? A satirical art project? Was some criminal mastermind taking over the stock market and gambling with everyone's money?

As public reports of the Call declined, the reach of this black stock market only grew. By the time Noa joined CSIS, terminating this underground insider trading ring was already a top priority for Canadian and American government organizations.

Their efforts, though, were disorganized and fruitless. With so many agencies carrying a stake, the levels of bureaucracy escalated at an exponential degree. The red tape frustrated Noa endlessly, and when he wormed his way into the insider trading meetings and got scolded because it 'wasn't his case,' he decided to abandon protocol.

His case pertained to the Great Lakes Collective, not the financial calls. But there was something too theatrical about the Call, he thought. Almost as if it was a marketing ploy to set up a new line of business for an existing criminal enterprise. One that was hell-bent on ensuring the quality of its 'products.'

He was certain this was work of the Niagara Company, but officially, the two were not connected and he was forbidden from interfering with the Call case.

A week into his employment, Noa was forced to reveal how he obtained the invaluable data on the Rideau-St. Lawrence mafia war, accessed CSIS private directories, and instigated what had come to be known internally as *The Tetris Incident* by spoofing a view of their intranet server with software he developed and stored on a little cube marked with an 11.

Only Director Colson and Agents Koven and Lavoie were present for the explanation. Everyone in the room signed a non-disclosure agreement swearing to secrecy, and Noa swearing never to repeat his actions. It took about six hours and two sessions to walk through a basic overview of their system's weak links and an introduction to the deep & dark web.

A month into his employment, Noa was back in the depths once more. Outside of work hours and on a mirrored operating system, he sat underneath a willow tree by the waterfront with his computer on his lap, searching for a connection.

The dark web is a galaxy of untouchable – well, mostly untouchable – sites whose IP addresses bounce off countless routers, making it the perfect tool for illegal activity. Noa knew this better than most, having used it to his advantage in his interview.

He just needed to find one connection. One mistake, one chain, linking the prophetical calls and trades with the elusive Niagara Co.

Noa knew the source of the Call wouldn't be shelling out investment advice for free. Once word got out that the advice was legit, surely a business plan would be activated. The only way to retain anonymity after that is online, through an onion router or something similar on deep web browsers.

The virtual browsers act as an invisibility cloak for internet users, as their computer's address bounces off international routers without a trace so many times that it's nearly impossible to track.

Nearly impossible.

Noa now had at his disposable a full arsenal of security software, borrowed without approval from his employers. And although internet activity was untraceable through onion routers, there was one piece of the puzzle that can't be covered up completely: payment.

Virtual currency, while protected by layers upon layers of encryption, keeping the buyers and sellers of illegal merchandise safe from prying eyes, must be linked to real currency at some point. A momentary crack in the shield.

Noa searched the hidden corners of online black-market forums for relevant keywords, matching the times of suspiciously successful aboveground stock market trades. Upon locating the trace of a couple payers, he followed the path of the money through the net. It took hours, but at last, he found a connection.

It was getting dark under the willow trees of the lakeshore Toronto park on that late autumn evening, when the lone, peculiar teenager pumped a fist in the air, dropping an unlit cigarette, and audibly shouted, "I got you!"

———

The following Monday, he was at a loss. The last time Noa tried joining the insider trading case, he got in trouble. And when he suggested using less-than legitimate means of proving his hypothetical connection, Agent Lavoie threatened to deport him.

Agents Lee and Sanders were too uptight, he thought. And Director Colson downright terrified him. It would have to be Agent Koven. He had a strong moral compass but also seemed to be the only one that didn't hate the new hire's guts.

Winter approached. Lost in contemplation, Noa stared into his cold cup of coffee one afternoon, planning how to broach the subject with his boss. After all, simply browsing the dark web for research isn't illegal, but that comes with a great big asterisk when you hijack government software to work on a case that's outside your bureaucratic mandate, especially when you're a teenage hacker that manipulated his way into a job by similar means.

"Are you trying to heat up that coffee with your stare? We have microwaves here in Canada, you know," Agent Koven had approached Noa's desk without him noticing and was watching him with some concern. "You alright?"

Noa blinked a few times, collecting his thoughts. Now or never. "Actually, Agent Koven, I was wondering if I could speak with you about our case."

Koven considered this, then looked at his watch. "How about we go for a coffee break?"

Noa looked at the older agent, then at his gloomy mug. "Okay, but I'd really like to discuss something with you," he said, following Koven out with his laptop under his arm.

They made their way to a local café and sat down with their drinks in a quiet spot under the canopy of a large indoor plant.

"Thanks for the coffee," Noa said quickly, placing his laptop on the table in between them. "So, about the case—"

"Noa," Koven interrupted. "How are you doing?"

Agent Koven was the only person in CSIS that called him by name. The rest would call him 'Sinclair,' or 'that exchange student,' or, his least favorite, 'Little Red.'

"I'm fine. Why?" he answered after a brief silence.

Koven leaned forward slightly, searching his eyes. A similar tactic to Director Colson, but not nearly as intimidating. "You're on my team now. I like to know how my agents are doing. I know you work long hours, even though you're so new. You shouldn't push yourself so hard."

Noa wondered if this was the same feigned politeness he'd come to know or genuine concern. "I'm quite used to working hard, sir."

"I can only imagine," Koven said softly. "It must be tough, settling in to a new country on your own. I know I'm your boss but if you ever need help or just to talk, you can reach out."

Noa wondered if there was some genuine concern there after all. "Thank you, sir."

"Alright, I'll stop pressing you," Koven raised his hands in mock surrender. "What've you got to show me?"

The boy nodded, pulling some screens up on the monitor. "It's about the insider trading."

Agent Koven sipped his coffee, "This again? I told you, the word from the top is that it's not our wheelhouse."

"I heard." Scrolling walls of text and a multitude of network windows reflected off of Noa's glasses. Koven watched him warily from the other side of the computer screen.

"Listen, I know you think the Niagara Company is responsible," the older agent said. "I wouldn't be surprised if you were right. But we are up to our necks dealing with them as it is. We'd need a massive budget to look into those investment calls, not to mention a way to connect them to the Collective. Honestly, we've been told to leave it to the feds down south—"

"Sir," Noa said hurriedly, "I found the connection." He finished setting up and removed a familiar, compact cube from his pocket.

Koven recognized the 11 insignia immediately. "Noa, no. Please tell me you didn't."

The redhead opted to disregard the comment and connected the cube. The 11 powered on with a white light.

"Noa, please," Agent Koven was staring right at him. "Consider what you're about to tell me. If you used illegal means to obtain this information, I will be forced to take action. The Director was very clear about your terms and conditions."

Noa avoided eye contact, building up resolve. "Just hear me out, sir. What they're doing, is, well," he clenched a fist unintentionally, "it's unbelievable. I'm just doing my job."

Koven rubbed his forehead with an open palm. "I will

probably regret this, but alright. Show me what you found, agent."

Excitedly, without pausing for breath unless absolutely necessary, Noa sped through his discovery. Koven moved his chair over to the other side of the table, following along as best as he could on the screen.

Traced calls and encrypted transactions, illicit forums used by drug dealers, black market sites selling weapons, confidential government files on economic movements. Koven watched with an anxious but curious expression.

"But this means the Great Lakes Collective..." Koven muttered under his breath.

"Exactly," Noa exclaimed proudly. "It's our case after all!"

Koven stood from the table. He was a few shades paler than before. "These are amazing findings. I can't condone your methods, but I also understand why you would go this far."

Noa shut his computer and put the 11-marked cube back in his pocket. "So, you agree! Now the cases can be combined, right? And our resources expanded?"

"I'll arrange a debrief," said Koven. "Still, Noa, listen carefully. Send this to me but keep it to yourself until I can think of a way to present your conclusions that won't get you imprisoned."

"Oh," the boy uttered. "Right."

He followed his boss back inside the CSIS building in awkward silence and didn't hear anything for days until a meeting was arranged between his team, the national white-collar crime team – which was tracking the insider trading calls – and the director.

It was a cloudy early winter morning. More than twenty people shuffled into a large conference room.

On one side of the table sat the financial and cyber-crime team for the border region: Noa, along with Agents Koven, Lavoie, Sanders and Lee. Across from them was a multitude of faces Noa did not recognize, likely partners from the US, and others from the CSIS insider trading case division. Director Colson entered the room and took a seat at the head of the table.

As the meeting attendees settled in, Noa couldn't help but recoil under the questioning glances of those around him. He tried to busy himself by focusing on the case information but found himself unable to concentrate.

Since his coffee break with Agent Koven, he hadn't heard any updates and wasn't sure what he was supposed to share at this meeting. There were so many people. The prospect of speaking in front of them petrified him. The murmurs of surrounding agents were drowned out by the deafening sound of his heartbeat.

He glanced over at Agent Koven but couldn't get a good view as Sanders and Lee were between them.

Director Colson cleared her throat.

"I believe we're all here, so let's get started," she said in a clear and resounding voice. Noa noticed that there were even more people dialed into the meeting through the phone.

"There is really just one matter on the agenda today and that is our involvement in the insider trading investigation," she continued. "I won't go through introductions, but we have our US counterparts joining us as well as the white-collar crime department, as these findings may result in the expansion of an existing team in our border crime division. With that, I will pass it over to Agent Alex Koven, the head of the Cybercrime Unit and Senior Canadian Intelligence Agent."

All attention shifted to Agent Koven as he stood. "Thank you, ma'am."

Agent Lavoie, who was seated on the other side of Koven, caught Noa's eye. She glared at him with such contempt that he genuinely shivered.

Koven powered on the projector and displayed an image linking various entities and tracing a number of activities to them. Noa recognized the work as his own, albeit significantly watered down to its simplest form.

"I'll provide some brief context for those I haven't met before," Koven said. "My team is currently tracking the mafia known as the Niagara Company, which is believed to be the largest and most powerful organization among a group of criminal syndicates we call the Great Lakes Collective."

There were some nods around the table.

"When incidents of the Call began in the summer of this year, we initially did not consider them to be related. However, we now know that they most definitely are." Koven said dryly.

The nods stopped. Noa looked around the room nervously.

"Now, hold on," a man with a grey tie and matching greying hair spoke up. "You're saying this Niagara group is placing the calls? Isn't that a bit of a reach? We're looking at the Fortune 500 channels and those with stock market know-how."

"Not only that," said another, this time a woman with round glasses. "But your slide there has the Call tracing to the Cicero Gang out of Chicago. That's Great Lakes Collective, but not Niagara Co."

A voice crackled on the conference phone, "Hi, this is Agent Singh from Quantico. How exactly did you trace this link from a call investor to the Great Lake group? Our folks have been on that day and night with no success." Clear disbelief hovered on the agent's tone.

"There was one more discovery that we made, which will clear some things up," said Koven. He flipped to another slide. "As you can see, the Great Lakes Collective *doesn't actually exist.* The Cicero Gang, the Cleveland-Pittsburgh Partnership, the Milwaukee Family, the Chicago Outfit, the Five Families in New York, and more: they're all shells."

Noa bit his lip, watching realization dawn across the faces of the agents in the room.

This time, Director Colson spoke up. "They're fronts of Niagara Co.? *All* of those mafia groups?"

"That's correct," Koven said with a curt nod. "They're not even puppets. They exist solely on paper. All this time we thought we were dealing with upwards of ten different criminal organizations, but it was only one. Working with unbelievable efficiency."

A man sitting close to the projector screen squinted at the results. "How did you get this information? This is unprecedented. It would mean they more than likely have the capability to be behind the insider trading—"

"I'm not convinced," said the voice on the phone. "Okay, sure, so our waterfall friends are more impressive than we thought. How do you figure they're behind the calls?"

Noa tightly gripped the handlebars of his chair, almost vibrating in anticipation.

Agent Koven changed the slide again. "All we had to find was one connection. One mistake in their flawless execution."

Noa was actually taken aback by the presentation of

data on the screen. He couldn't have said it better himself. In fact, he almost wished he could have. After all, now Agent Koven was taking the credit for his work.

"Think of the initial calls as a 'proof of concept,' in marketing terms," Koven went on. "Those were the calls that Niagara Co. allowed to be covered by the media and didn't expect anything in return. Then, the volume drastically decreased, and the publicity stopped. But those that needed to know about their new business venture, did."

"You're saying they sell insider information?" asked a woman on the phone. "Why? Wouldn't it be more profitable to bet on the market themselves since they have the info?"

"Their business model is more intricate than that," said Koven. "Once the quality of their product was established, they set up an investment firm-type operation, and massive amounts of interested investors bought into their guaranteed-to-shoot-up funds. And for Niagara Co., the profit was and is exponential."

Director Colson whistled, "That's quite a finding, Alex. How do investors buy-in?" She posed her question to the agent but made brief eye contact with Noa.

The teenager swallowed uncomfortably.

"Yes, ma'am," Koven clicked forward to an appendix slide. "To put it simply, they pay online. But the reason it works is because they operate through encrypted currency transactions on the dark web."

A few agents looked at the information in front of them dubiously.

Koven continued, "However, while these transactions are untraceable through router cloaking, there was one instance we were able to trace. Just as the calls began, there was one payment traced from an investment call that used the same channel as a Cicero Gang heroin purchase."

"Which means—" Agent Singh said barely audibly.

"Since Niagara Co. *is* the Cicero Gang, we can only conclude that one of their customers, eager to buy into the new investment fund, combined their capital with their payment for a drug deal." Koven said with an exhale. "Two birds; one stone."

Director Colson was silent, studying the screenshots of the dark web entanglement on the screen. Her face did not betray any signs of emotion.

"Agent Koven," said a voice on the phone, "Chief Hastings of the FBI. This is exemplary work. If this is accurate, I look forward to our teams working together on this case so we can finally get to the bottom of their insider sources. However, I'm very interested – how did you access this data? Assuming you didn't surf the deep web yourself!" He added with a chuckle.

A man in a beige suit gaped at the conference phone with bulging eyes. "Greg Walchuck, Chief Security Officer. Please, sir, we take security risk and cyber ethics very seriously at CSIS. Our agents abide by laws and regulations in all their investigations."

"I would hope so," the FBI chief said over the phone. "I'm not sure about you guys and the Mounties, but down here that would result in swift disciplinary action."

Noa no longer wished he was presenting. He felt a massive pit of nerves collecting in his stomach as he looked up at Agent Koven. He wasn't entirely certain but he could have sworn that the agent gave him a quick, reaffirming wink.

"Before we go on," Director Colson said, standing from her seat, "I would just like to make sure we are all aligned.

Agent Koven: You have demonstrated to us in no uncertain terms that not only is the Great Lakes Collective a sham that operates entirely under the Niagara Co., but also that Niagara Co. is the source of the insider trading calls. Do we agree?"

A series of nods rippled around the table, and reluctant affirmations sounded on the phone.

"Fantastic. That means our next steps are to consolidate our task forces and establish a home base and operational team, targeting this larger entity," she said firmly.

A silence in the room confirmed her call-to-action.

"In that case," the director continued, "I would now like to ask everyone to leave the room and conference line except for Agent Koven's current team and our Chief Security Officer."

As murmurs erupted around him, this was the moment Noa understood how screwed he truly was. He affixed his gaze to his lap, folding his hands together nervously.

"Director Cols—" an objection was raised from the conference phone, but quickly muted.

"We will be in touch shortly to answer any follow-up questions," she said. "I appreciate your time. I'm hanging up now."

Seeing that she was serious, the rest of the attendees filed out of the room once Director Colson turned off the conference phone. A few of them shot accusatory glances at Agent Koven. A few were those of pity.

Noa thought he might pass out. His clenched hands were starting to turn white.

Director Colson sat down again once there were only seven people in the room: her, Agents Koven, Lavoie, Sanders and Lee, Greg Walchuck, and Noa. Koven was still standing by the projector.

"Madam Director," Greg began, "What is the meaning of this?"

"Alex, would you like to explain? Or should I?" Director Colson leaned back. "Or perhaps Agent Sinclair would like to share with the class?"

Noa's heart skipped a beat. He unfurled his hands and started to stand but was stopped by Koven's outstretched arm.

"No need, ma'am," said Koven. "Agent Sinclair had nothing to do with this."

Noa felt himself drop back down into his chair. From his periphery, he could feel Agent Lavoie's glare once again.

"You're saying you used CSIS resources and software to legally obtain this information? Information that our colleagues with massively larger budgets could only dream of obtaining?" Colson asked, voice dripping with sarcasm.

Greg, the Security Officer, clicked his pen over and over, "Ma'am, are you implying—"

"I got the information that was necessary to pursue and investigate this case, by the means that were available to me," said Koven. "Outside of CSIS work hours, and using a mirrored operating system, I accessed certain sites on the dark web. And I used replicas of CSIS software to trace the data I needed, without my superiors' knowledge or approval."

"Unthinkable!" Greg exclaimed, dropping his pen. "Inexcusable! For a senior agent, a division head to engage in such activity."

"Yes," Director Colson said, looking directly at Noa. "It is unthinkable. I would never expect such a thing from you, Alex. If you truly did this, you understand what it means, don't you?"

Noa couldn't bear to look up. He felt crushed by the

weight of his naivety and guilt. With a weak voice he managed to say, "Um, I—"

"These actions were mine and mine alone, ma'am," Koven said firmly. "No other member of my team holds any responsibility."

Noa lifted his head to see Agent Koven standing straight, facing the director and Security Officer head-on with a steely resolve. His respect for his boss grew ten times that day.

"Fine, if you want to play it that way, Alex." Director Colson said finally. "We'll talk tomorrow about the repercussions of your actions. You may go."

Following that meeting, the next couple months were a whirlwind of activity.

Much to Noa's relief, Agent Koven kept his job. He wasn't sure about the repercussions, but he did notice a decline in the quality of the agent's suits. Noa thanked Koven profusely, but he just told him to stay out of trouble and keep up the good work.

On the flip side, much to Noa's dismay, the new task-force for dealing with the transnational entity of Niagara Co. was huge, and his team grew proportionally. The number of people calling him 'Little Red' increased each week as well.

Nevertheless, the boost in resources was helpful to their cause, and Noa continued his investigation into the elusive Niagara Co. with a reignited enthusiasm. With access to better software, he didn't need to rely on illegal means of obtaining data. At least, not as much. He soon made another significant discovery about those prophetical phone calls.

Having gathered months and months of call and investment data since the summer of 2013, Noa was finally able to pinpoint the origin call. The 'patient zero,' so to speak.

The insider trading started in Toronto.

This revelation earned Noa some praise, as a higher budget got allocated to the Canada-based team. Still, he couldn't quite understand the appeal. Why start there?

Unless, he thought, *the Niagara Co. was based in Canada at the time.*

The theory hit him like a brick. It was very likely. After all, if the Niagara Co. operated out of Niagara Falls, Lake Ontario sat on the New York-Ontario border. The Bay Street stock exchange is not a bad place to try out a new business if you're not on Wall Street.

On the morning of February 7th, Noa paced around the top floor of the CSIS building. His team got moved up to the nicest view once it expanded, which was a blessing during the winter because all you could really do with the outdoors was look at it.

The sun had risen, but it was still early. The DOS screen with the clearance level three file shone on his monitor.

Where are you, he thought to himself, *and how can I find you?* He sat back down and started listing through all the known documentation on the Niagara Co.'s front corporations. On a secondary monitor, he pulled up the information on the origin calls.

Something must have changed for you, he reasoned as he typed, *when you started insider trading. That's quite a strategic shift for a mafia equivalent of a conglomerate. Which of your shells faltered? Which of them changed?*

The answer soon revealed itself, now that he knew what he was looking for. Two businesses, tied one way or another to the Niagara Co., popped up in the summer of 2013, in Niagara Falls, of all places: A winery and an ice cream parlor.

Noa's eyes lit up.

He flipped a coin. "Ice cream it is."

Using his CSIS corporate card, he purchased a train ticket to Niagara Falls.

And left.

SIX

OLD YORK TRIBUNE

- Toronto. October 10, 2012 -

No one knows how long this particular copy of the Old York Tribune existed in our world. No one knows if it is the only one of its kind. For weeks, it was in the possession of a homeless man and used as a makeshift blanket together with countless other newspapers on the concrete of Downtown Toronto.

The Tribune's previous owner had stopped before this homeless man one moonlit evening and handed him the rolled-up newspaper.

"Whassat?" The man asked, eyeing the stranger apprehensively.

"Check out the editorial on page 10," the stranger replied in a voice that sounded neither male nor female. "It'll change your life."

As the stranger walked away, the man on the sidewalk flipped to the tenth page.

Have you ever experienced a premonition? The inexplicable feeling that *something* was about to happen, and then it did? Or how about an overwhelming sense of *déjà-vu*? When you were convinced that an exact scenario has happened before, and you're reliving it anew? It's a strange and unsettling feeling, but not uncommon.

How about a vivid dream or nightmare foretelling the events of the following day with frightening accuracy?

Humankind has been hypothesizing about visions of the future as long as the idea of the "future" has existed. A fascinating concept that's captured the hearts of many: conjuring what lies ahead. Prophesying. Divination.

Science assures us that these phenomena are just a result of our primitive brains correcting their own errors. A synapse fired too soon here, a memory processed too slow there, and voila.

Preachers would like us to believe that these glimpses of the future are divine messages from deities or angels, warning us of things to come.

And who knows, maybe there's an X-file or two, documenting truly psychic individuals, hidden away in underground archives.

But the truth of the matter is, *it's something else.*

Something without a form that ebbs and flows in the gaps between realities. The darkest corners where our collective conscious existence meets the next. The in-between. A jumbled mess of time and space, spinning haphazardly in every direction at once.

And sometimes, it leaks.

For the most part, it's nothing serious. Humans think they've figured out how to measure time, but time is immeasurable. True, time can only flow forwards, but at various speeds. It can skip. It can hasten. It can slow down.

It can leak.

Again, for the most part, the only consequence is a weird

sensation in the back of your mind or a nagging feeling that
you've seen this before or know what's about to happen.
But sometimes, rarely, it leaks into the physical plane.
Sometimes, something slips between the cracks.
Sometimes, it ends up in the wrong reality.
Interested in learning more? Call us at:

The number had been torn off.

Confused and slightly irritated, the homeless man
tossed the newspaper onto the pavement along with his
other belongings and forgot about the editorial entirely.

One cold October day, desperate for a break in the
tedium of his daily routine, he decided to read the papers on
which he slept before the morning commute began. He
didn't usually wake up this early, but the wind was exceptionally harsh that morning.

The man, whose name was Sid, wasn't particularly good
at reading. But he enjoyed the comic strips, the sports
columns, and checking the week's weather on the front
page. Anything to pass the time.

As he sat on the pavement, skimming the tattered pages,
the bells of the St. James Cathedral started to toll their holy
call.

One chime, two...

The rush hour will be peaking soon, he thought, as he
flipped the page.

Three chimes, four...

The Old York Tribune was a nice publication, but this
paper had seen better days. It was ripping at the corners and
slightly damp from the pavement. Luckily, it was still
legible.

Five chimes, six, seven...

Sid had never bothered checking the date on the front

page. Why would he ever think to do so? It didn't matter anyway, because he was up early today.

Today, he decided to read the paper.

Eight.

Today, as the eighth bell tolled, Sid witnessed a wonder beyond comprehension.

All at once, the printed letters started to dance on the pages. Ink swirled across the columns, forming new words and numbers in a matter of seconds. The paragraphs waged a tiny revolution. The text defied its creators and sought new existence.

At eight in the morning of October 10th, a homeless man named Sid saw a vision of October 11th on the off-white print pages of an unremarkable newspaper.

His first thought was that of amazement. His second was that of terror. He dropped the paper, hastily jumping to his feet. He stared at the Old York Tribune in distress, unable to move.

The wind was picking up, threatening to carry the spell-binding newspaper into traffic. At the prospect of losing it, Sid gingerly picked up the paper again, studying its contents. No doubt, he was hallucinating. Surely, the words didn't actually move. Obviously.

Sid's tired eyes caught sight of the date. Tomorrow's date.

And then, as if a lightbulb sparked to life above his head, he flipped to the sports pages.

Grinning like a madman, Sid practically skipped all the way to the stadium. He knew a number of bookies from his past, before he gambled away his earnings into obscurity. In a twist a fate, the same vice that destroyed him would save him from poverty.

After begging an old friend to front him a bit of cash,

Sid bet the entire amount on the Maple Leafs. This was a risky move – they were playing the Boston Bruins tonight. But Sid didn't falter in his choice. He decided to place the utmost trust in his newspaper. He had nothing to lose.

The city of Toronto was in an excited uproar that night when their team beat Boston for the first time in years. A close game. Just as the Old York Tribune's sports columnist predicted.

On the following day, Sid watched the letters on the front page rearrange again, a ritual that would soon become religious. ***Toronto homeless man wins $5 million lottery*** read the headline. With the details of his day spelled out in black and white, he thanked his lucky stars and rushed to the convenience store.

Sid, formerly homeless, accumulated wealth at a staggering pace. He soon had to stop buying lottery tickets as some in the press became suspicious of his success. But, hooked on the thrill, he continued to use the newspaper to make money on bets where he could.

Afraid of being discovered, he locked himself away in a lavish suburban villa, leaving only for necessities and gambling prospects, receding into the life of a paranoiac.

His paranoia was not unwarranted.

While his acquaintances brushed his good luck off as mere coincidence, the underworld took notice.

- Toronto. January, 2013 -

At the turn of the new year, four people met over steaming cups of recently boiled tea in a floating office.

Once temperatures dipped below freezing, boats typically vanished from the waterways of Lake Ontario and took up their hibernation in marinas and docks along the harbors.

Yet one yacht sailed into Ashbridges Bay on the East end of the Toronto waterfront, bearing a glossy white design and embossed lettering identifying her as *Aurora III*.

"Crisse qu'y fait frette!" A well-dressed man with a French accent and shiny bald head pressed his hands to the hot porcelain of his teacup. "I appreciate you taking the time, Sebastian, but we really could have met in my office here, or in Montréal."

Behind the boat's wheel, Mike made a show of increasing the heat. "The Boss prefers the waves!"

Sebastian, unbothered by the cold, gazed out the cabin's window. "I meet most of my clients like this, Francois. Unless it is a meeting from which my guest does not return," he said casually.

"What they say is true," Francois chuckled. "Millennial Tycoon, they call you."

"How patronizing," Sebastian frowned. "So, to what do I owe the pleasure of meeting Monsieur Dorval of the Notre Dame casino dynasty?" He turned back to face the bald man and the one sitting beside him – a mousy accountant with oversized glasses and a perpetually worried expression.

Francois Dorval, a French-Canadian gangster backing the largest gambling rings in Quebec and Ontario, elbowed his bookkeeper in the side.

"*Sacrament*, Michel," Francois swore under his breath. "You sent the file, *non?*"

The nervous little man nodded vigorously, *"Oui*, yes, this morning!"

Sebastian took up his tea with some consideration. "Forgive me, but I was under the impression that the memo you sent me this morning must have been a farce, or a code of some kind. Which is why I'm curious to know the real reason behind our rendezvous."

Michel the accountant ceased nodding and started to shake his head. *"Non,* not a farce," he said, pulling out an array of papers and spreading them haphazardly on the table.

"He's right," Francois added, reaching into his suit pocket and withdrawing a cigar. "Mind if I smoke?"

Sebastian's grip on the teacup tightened. "Yes, I mind. You can do that onshore."

"Ah, fine," Francois waved the cigar in the air. "Later."

As the mess of papers swelled in front of him, Sebastian placed his free hand down atop the pile.

"I read your file," he said with a hint of agitation. "Let me confirm that we are on the same page. You think some hermit on a hill is running a one-man gambling op?"

"I know how it sounds, Sebastian. But I wouldn't ask for your services if I didn't think something odd was happening," said the bald man.

Although primarily a criminal by trade, Sebastian had a peculiar knack for investigating. Perhaps it was thanks to his background, but his past was not a topic to be discussed. Clients and allies soon recognized his keen intellect, and it offered the young outlaw no lack of interesting problems to solve when he was bored.

"So, do you think you can handle this or *non?"* Francois asked, twirling the unlit cigar in his fingers. "If not, I can ask somebody else."

"I'm assuming you've already tried," Sebastian remarked, earning him an irritated glare from the Frenchman.

Michel was tugging at some photographs that were

caught under Sebastian's hand. "Our people followed him, tapped his phones, spied on him – everything! We can't figure it out."

Sebastian moved his hand and watched Michel align pictures of an odd, middle-aged man in chronological order with piquing curiosity. "Your file mentioned he got rich from betting on the racetrack on the books and sports off the books. What does he do before placing a bet?"

"*Et Voila*! Nothing!" The bookkeeper gestured emphatically to the stills on the table. "He consults no one. He doesn't use the internet to research anything. He just wakes up, has his breakfast, reads the paper, and drives over to the bookies to place his bets. *C'est bizarre*."

"Bad for business," Francois muttered.

Sebastian studied the photos. "He does not look like the type to be involved in a covert gambling operation."

"Word on the street is that he used to be, how do you say? *Un clochard*," Michel said.

"Homeless? You don't say," Sebastian placed his tea down on the collection of photographs. "Alright, I'll look into him. But what exactly do you want me to do, Francois?"

Francois shrugged, "I'll leave the details to you, Monsieur Tycoon. Just get rid of him. Find out how he does it or don't, *je m'en fiche*. I'm not the only one inconvenienced. If you sort this out for me, my contacts will know."

Sebastian smiled, standing from the table. "Consider him gone."

As *Aurora III's* guests disembarked on Woodbine beach, Sebastian met Mike at the bow of the yacht.

"I really hate that nickname," he said.

"I think it sounds cool!" Mike offered with a grin. "So, what do you think, Boss? This hobo some kind of psychic?"

Sebastian gazed up at the sky, silver clouds beckoning snow to fall. "If he's found some way to see the future, I pity him. Deep in the man sits fast his fate, to mold his fortunes, mean or great."

Mike nodded in contemplation. "Shakespeare?"

"Emerson. In any case," Sebastian added, "I need to do some independent research on our prosperous friend. You can return to home base; I'll take the Aurora when I'm done."

"You got it, Boss."

Over the next week, Sebastian compiled all available data on the formerly homeless man named Sid. He moved around a few times before settling into a mansion in the extravagant Bridle Path neighborhood of North York.

Calling it a mansion, though, didn't do the house justice. It was more of an isolated castle, fenced off with pines, in the most upscale community in the city.

But other than getting insanely rich insanely fast, there was nothing significant or out of place about the man. Sebastian's curiosity grew.

On a Tuesday afternoon in January, he headed North.

The snow had finally stopped falling when he reached the luxurious villa. Careful to avoid suspicion, Sebastian took the train uptown and made his way to the house on foot.

He couldn't help but be amused by the sight before him. The house unmistakably belonged to a nutcase. Multiple scarecrows littered the front lawn, along with months' worth of decaying leaves and trash.

Sebastian circled the perimeter of the house, looking for

a way in. The front door was padlocked, indicating the owner wasn't home. This was a rare opportunity, considering how infrequently he left. The windows were boarded up from the inside and the cellar door was shut tight. No luck with the back doors either.

Sebastian glanced upward with a sigh. His best bet was the chimney.

Although he was in good shape, the young man had a difficult time climbing up to the roof. The mansion's exterior was slippery, and the brick was uncooperative for traction.

Once he finally made it to the chimney, he peered down. It was about a 15-foot drop. If he was careful, he could slide down without incident.

But he was not careful.

With a harsh thud, Sebastian landed, rear-first, on the pile of wood in the fireplace. Getting up carefully and wiping the soot off his backside, he peered around the living room for any signs of life. Welcomed by silence, he began his search.

Sebastian wasn't sure what he was looking for, but he figured something must be out of place.

The mansion's interior was unremarkable. It was filled with high-tech toys and expensive trinkets that a newly rich person would purchase and never use.

The coffee table caught Sebastian's eye. It was plain, mahogany wood. Ordinary. However, on a barely visible shelf underneath it, protected on all sides by clear plastic film, sat a newspaper.

He just wakes up, has his breakfast, reads the paper, and leaves.

Sebastian picked it up without much deliberation. He froze when he noticed tomorrow's date on the front page.

The headline read: *83 people dead, 150 injured in rocket attack – Aleppo University. Syrian Civil War wages on.* Midway through the page, there was a story about the discovery of horse meat in UK supermarket burgers, and another about the Russians launching satellites to space.

Entranced, he turned the page. Local Canadian news about the Prime Minister's new venture capital plan. Political clashes between the two major parties. A hockey doctor slandered for lying about swine flu vaccines. Sports updates on national winners.

He turned to the third page.

Bridle Path mansion ravaged by fire: One unidentified man dead, read the headline. There was a photo underneath the title. Sebastian recognized the charred scarecrows immediately.

"It can't be," he whispered to himself in disbelief.

Sebastian stumbled back against the coffee table when he heard the padlock clicking open. Without a second thought, he stuffed the newspaper under his jacket and hid in the front closet.

Keeping completely still, he watched through a crack in the shutters as the front door swung open and the homeowner stepped inside. He was holding a small plastic bag and was muttering aloud.

"Ain't no way I'm dying today, oh no." Sid slammed the door shut and emptied the contents of the bag into his hand. It was just one item.

Sebastian squinted to make out the object. A box of matches.

"I know I can't control fate, O Holy One," Sid said frantically, raising his hands up to the sky. "This place will burn, that is your will, but I won't be the one to die!"

Sebastian watched with nervous anticipation as the man paced the room.

Sid checked his watch, giggling to himself. "That delivery guy will be here soon, yes, and he won't be leaving. I'll make sure he stays. It's him in the paper, yes, not me!"

Planning a murder because of a newspaper? He figured Sid truly was unhinged.

Suddenly, Sebastian's eyes widened in horror as he felt a familiar vibration tingling in his back pocket.

♪ *Fly me to the moon, let me play among the stars* ♪

Sinatra's melodic voice rang out from the behind the closet door.

♪ *Let me see what spring is like on a-Jupiter and Mars* ♪

Cursing himself for forgetting to mute his cellphone, Sebastian braced for impact.

Sid tore open the closet door, nearly ripping it clean off.

"WHO ARE YOU?" His voice boomed with a crazed fury.

Sebastian considered his options but did not have a chance to answer as Sid went on.

"Wait, wait," he mumbled, "No, no, this is perfect!"

With a mighty force, Sid shoved Sebastian further into the closet. When his back hit the wall, Sid slammed the door shut and pushed a chair up against the handles.

"Now I don't even have to wait for the delivery guy!" Sid laughed. "You'll do just fine, young fella!"

Shit, Sebastian thought, pushing at the door. It wouldn't budge.

"Oh divine, judgement day," Sid hollered triumphantly.

Sebastian tensed when he heard a match being struck. His mind raced. As he struggled with the door, he felt an irritating tickle against his stomach.

"Ah," Sebastian cleared his throat, "my friend, you might not want to do anything hasty."

"It's too late, boy!" Sid tapped on the closet door mockingly. "Can't you *smell it?*"

He could. Sebastian coughed from the smoke that was gathering in the room but continued. "You're going to leave your precious oracle to burn here with me?"

Sid's laughter stopped abruptly. Sebastian could hear him scrambling to the coffee table and subsequently running back to the closet.

"You have it! **YOU TOOK IT**!" he shouted, banging on the door.

"Indeed, I have it right here." Sebastian removed the plastic casing and crinkled the pages for Sid to hear. "What now?"

"GIVE IT BACK! GIVE IT BACK, GIVE IT BACK, GIVE IT BACK, **GIVE IT BACK!**" the crazy man bellowed, continuously pounding on the door.

The living room was already ablaze, flames eating away at the wooden boards covering the windows. Breathable air was becoming scarce.

Sebastian quietly removed a wire coat hanger from above him and untwisted it. "Well, I can't give it back unless you open the door, wouldn't you say?"

Sid was furious. Heat from the flames and anger impaired his increasingly shaky judgement. He moved the chair aside and the instant that followed was all Sebastian needed.

He kicked open the door and, in the blink of an eye, the sharp bronze end of the coat hanger impaled Sid through the chest.

The fire spread to the walls. Hearing the creaking of the foundation, Sebastian pushed the astonished man aside and bolted. As Sid fell back, Sebastian jumped through the first-story window, clutching the newspaper safely under his arm.

Not a minute later, the luxurious mansion collapsed in a fiery heap.

Taking a few steps back on the front lawn, Sebastian dropped to the ground in a coughing fit. The flames enveloped the house so fast that Sid didn't have time to scream.

Sebastian stood slowly, inhaling all the oxygen his lungs could take. Without another glance, he made his way downtown. It would be a while before the fire department arrived, and the body in the villa would not be identified, just as the news from January 15 had predicted.

For the next few weeks, Sebastian kept the *Aurora* anchored in Toronto's harbor, examining the newspaper.

On his way back to the port, he bought numerous copies of Old York Tribunes from different sources and picked up some old ones – from subway station shops, convenience stores, street corner kiosks. He lined the main cabin of the yacht with Tribunes, computer screens, and whiteboards, transforming it into a floating quasi-laboratory.

Comparing his acquired copy of the Tribune with the others, it was clear that it was identical in every way. Except, there was the matter of the 8 o'clock metamorphosis.

Sebastian didn't know what else to call it. On the second morning, he noticed the change occurring. Barring the title, all other little letters shifted around like inky ballerinas on the page, settling into the comfort of the following day's top stories in a matter of moments. He was mesmerized.

Each day, Sebastian tracked every report, every column, every prediction, and checked the results on the subsequent day. He also ran a series of experiments on the paper itself, documenting his findings with a scientific curiosity.

The whiteboard overflowed with his results.

Observation 1: Damage & Alterations

Test 1.1: Page A11 torn slightly (1") on the upper right-hand corner

Result: Tear remained thereafter **paramount to keep paper safe**

Test 1.2: Coffee spill on page A3, left-hand (sports column)

Result: Stain faded as time progressed – completely gone in 96 hours

Test 1.3: Crossword on page A6 filled out with ballpoint pen

Result: No evidence of pen markings 24 hours later

notes OK

Observation 2: Timing

• Content updates at 0800 EST every morning, captures following 24 hrs.

• Doesn't alter throughout the day **midday fluctuations not captured**

• Updates every day of the week (weekends included)

• Exception: Page 10 editorial does not change... why?

• What if paper is beyond Tribune's range? **TBD... need to test... Italy?**

Observation 3: Prediction Accuracy

• The Newspaper is **always** correct

It was February 12th when Sebastian called his team.

"Hey Boss!" Mike answered the phone, "Are you finally comin' back to us?"

"Not yet," Sebastian held the Tribune folded in one hand, phone in the other. "Can you put Elli on the line?"

Sounds of muffled shouts and some movement, then a familiar melodic voice.

"What can I do for you, Bassie?"

Sebastian's eye twitched at the name, "Don't call me that. How are things?"

"Hm," Elli sounded disappointed, "you're just calling for a status report? You know I'd tell you if anything was wrong, sugar." The sound of a notebook being opened. "The Rainbow Bridge consolidation is going smoothly. Seattle horses came quiet, and the Reservations across Montana followed suit when we offered the Great Lake deal in exchange as planned."

"Good," Sebastian said, "then do you have time for a quick assignment?"

"Assignment? I hope you're not asking me to kill anyone – you've got Luce for that," she said.

"No, nothing like that. I want to coordinate a large-scale stock purchase of two particular companies' shares."

"Oh, sure enough," she said. "New York Stock-Ex? NASDAQ? Which tickers, how many, and when do you want them purchased?"

"It must be done today, Elli," he said. "In the next couple hours. CMCSA on NASDAQ; GE on NYSE. As many shares as you can without raising alerts."

Elli hesitated. "So soon? I don't know, Bassie. I can do it, but the best dummy accounts I've got for an op this fast and large are local IPs I set up when I worked on Bay St. No one'll trace it back to us, but it won't be as diluted as it can be."

"It's fine," he said. "As long as it gets done before 4:00 PM today."

On the business column page of the Old York Tribune in his hand, dated February 13, 2013, was the following article:

Old York Tribune

FEBRUARY 13 2013

Comcast announces plans to buy General Electric's stake in NBCUniversal for $16.7B

By EDWARD CHOI
4:52PM EST

Comcast said Tuesday that it's buying the rest of NBCUniversal from General Electric for $16.7 billion, doing so several years early as the cable TV provider takes advantage of low borrowing costs and what CEO Brian Roberts called a "very attractive price."

Comcast's stock (NASDAQ: CM-CSA) jumped over 25 percent, to $71.46 in after-hours trading, following the announcement. GE (NYSE: GE) shares rose 7.6 percent, to $33.39.

"It's an attractive price - Comcast is getting a good deal," Wunderlich Securities analyst Matthew Harrigan said.

LONG-HELD AMBITIONS

Comcast turned its attention to NBC after a failed $54 billion hostile takeover attempt of Disney in 2004 that ultimately led to the resignation of that company's CEO, Michael Eisner, after more than 20 years on the job.

RELATED COVERAGE

NBC deal could push GE shares to highest since financial crisis The hostile offer exposed Comcast's desire to merge content with distribution at a time when most of its industry peers, such as Viacom-CBS and AOL-Time Warner, were doing the opposite.

While Comcast held the title of the nation's leading cable operator by a wide margin, its status as a content player was always second tier, with middling networks like E!, G4 and Golf forming the basis of its channel portfolio.

The NBC deal gave the Philadelphia-based cable operator

couped more profits earned by GE Capital.

COMCAST EARNINGS

In addition to the GE deal, Comcast reported fourth-quarter earnings on Tuesday.

It posted $15.94 billion in revenue, up 6 percent from a year ago. It posted net income of $1.5 billion, or 56 cents per share, up from $1.56 billion, or 47 cents a year ago.

In its cable business, it lost a net 7,000 video customers, which is better than the 17,000 subscribers lost a year ago.

Analysts said Comcast was getting a good deal at that price, while Comcast's chief executive said the company moved because it was eager to take control of the business sooner than planned.

"Okay," Elli said, "It'll be done before 4 o'clock! So, why are we buying Comcast stock?"

"Trying out a new venture," Sebastian said. "If this works, it'll open up some new capital for our expansion strategy."

"Gotcha. Well hurry on home, it's weird without you.

I'll let you know when the stocks are bought. Tootles!" Elli hung up.

A person could do great feats with the future in their hands. They could become a famous fortune-teller, or a prophet. They could try their luck at preventing terrible tragedies by warning the world of events to come.

That evening, once it became clear that Elli's multiple portfolios grew their share of Comcast and GE stock, Sebastian set the Niagara Co.'s newest revenue stream into motion.

SEVEN

POLAR PARLOR

- Toronto. February 7, 2014 -

"Isn't it just semantics, Miriam? Insider trading is insider trading."

"I'm saying this goes beyond insider trading, Alex. And even if it is insider trading, it's simply impossible for this lone syndicate, now that we know they *are* lone, to have so much information."

"Don't you mean improbable? They could have dozens, no, hundreds of informants in hundreds of companies feeding them information."

"Watch your rook, Alex." Agent Lavoie slid a black chess piece diagonally across the board. "Check."

"Damn." Agent Koven moved his white king out of harm's way.

The two agents met every Friday in Agent Koven's office for their weekly morning ritual – a friendly chess match, over which they would debate a case or discuss current events.

"What I'm saying is," Agent Lavoie continued, picking

up a black knight and stroking its rigid ivory mane, "the scope is too broad and the stock movements too extensive. They would need to have informants in *every* company around the world, apprising them of every miniscule organizational change or merger."

"I suppose that is highly unlikely," Agent Koven conceded. "But that's still insider trading, even though we can't prove how they're doing it. Yet."

"You're right," Lavoie placed her knight on the board. "But is that all they're doing?"

"What do you mean?" Koven responded by capturing her knight with a bishop.

"Market manipulation," she said, removing the bishop with her second knight. "I've been looking into the trends beyond company stock fluctuations on the main exchanges. Consider for a second that Niagara Co. is trading in gold, oil, or other commodities. Or in currencies."

Koven stared at the checkered board. "How could they be doing that?" He moved his queen to corner her king. "Check. I don't suppose you have any evidence of this?"

She moved a rook in front of her king. "June 2013, the first instance. The value of the US dollar jumped over 50% against the Canadian dollar. Within about an hour, the two-thirds of the gain was gone. Same pattern repeated in late August, only with 14 different currencies. Same thing: sharp spike followed by quick reversal."

Koven studied the board. "You think they knew in advance which currencies would trade favorably and told their investors? Who in turn exchanged the money in advance and cashed out the following day? How is that possible?"

"It's not," she said. "Unless they're manipulating the market. Check-mate, by the way."

"God damn it," Koven groaned. "I never win."

Lavoie shrugged. "In chess, as in life, it's best to think a few steps ahead. This Niagara Co. is more devious than I initially thought. They must have access to unimaginable financial networks or political ties that can gently sway the market for them without crashing it."

"Or some kind of magic wand," Koven sighed, stretching his arms. "If we crack this case, we'll make history."

"*When.*" Lavoie corrected, packing up the chess pieces.

"Right," he said. "Coffee?"

Before Lavoie could respond, there was a knock at the door.

"Expecting someone?" she asked. "It's so early. The pipsqueak?"

"You really ought to learn his name," Koven chided. "Come in."

Agent Lee opened the office door and stepped inside, looking down nervously. "Good morning sir. Ma'am."

"Morning, Lee," Koven said. "What's up? Everything alright?"

"Actually sir," the timid agent spoke softly, "I wasn't sure if I should bring this up, or to whom. It's kind of sensitive information."

"Well, out with it!" Lavoie sat up, leaning her elbows on the closed chessboard.

Agent Lee winced. "It's, um. It's about Agent Sinclair, sir."

"Oh? Now I'm especially intrigued," Lavoie said. "What did the little brat do now?"

"Miriam." Koven shot her a look.

"What? He's your employee but I'm his superior too. Whatever Lee has to say, I can hear it," she said.

"Just hold your judgement," he said. "I'll decide if we need to take the matter to Director Colson or anywhere else. Go ahead, Lee."

Agent Lee looked a bit distraught. "Well, like I said, it's a bit sensitive. But considering all of those code of conduct and employee training modules we had to complete before year-end, I figured I had to tell someone."

"This sounds serious," Koven frowned.

"A few days ago, I had to come back to the office after hours because I forgot some tickets in my drawer. It was almost nine, but Sinclair was still here. He had fallen asleep in one of the agile pods by the window, you know, the ones with the couch-like benches," Lee said.

Lavoie and Koven exchanged amused glances.

"Is that all?" Koven asked. "Noa frequently works late."

"No, sorry, that's not it," Lee said hurriedly. "Actually, I know I shouldn't have done this, but I came up to the floor with my girlfriend, since I was just grabbing the tickets. But she saw Sinclair and went to go check on him, thinking he was just someone's kid."

"Go on," Koven urged.

"Emily, um, that's my girlfriend, she leaned over to nudge him awake, but she noticed something. Sinclair had fallen asleep kind of draped over the pod table and the back of his sweater rode up." Lee hesitated. "Emily waved me over so I could see too. It looked like his back was covered with burns. Like, intentionally inflicted burn scars."

"What?" Koven stood. "Are you serious?"

Lee nodded. "Emily wanted to call child protective services, but I told her he worked with me. She couldn't believe it. We woke him up finally and he just said he zoned out while researching and went home. We felt too awkward bringing it up."

"Did the burns look recent?" Koven asked.

"I don't know," Lee said. "I wasn't sure who to bring this up to. I thought about it for a couple days and Emily kept urging me to at least tell my boss."

"You did the right thing, Lee." Koven said. "We need to make sure Noa is safe. Speaking of which, have you seen him this morning?"

"No sir," said Lee.

- Niagara Falls. February 7, 2014 -

Noa hopped off the train at the Niagara Falls Station, still riding the adrenaline surge of his impromptu decision. He had nothing with him except his backpack and the coordinates of the Polar Parlor. With growing anticipation and numbness from the cold, Noa hailed a cab.

"Old Falls and 1st Street, please," he said to the driver.

As the taxi made its way along the scenic parkway, Noa stared out the window at the raging Niagara river. He made a mental note to return to the falls at a nicer time of year.

The car stopped in front of a charming two-story brick building.

"That'll be twenty bucks, kid."

Noa handed him the money through the seats.

"You're on the US side now, kiddo. Canadian money won't fly here," the driver said.

"Oh, right." Noa stuffed the bill back into his wallet. "I'll do credit then."

After paying, Noa got out of the cab and stood in front of the Polar Parlor.

The picturesque shop, adorned with snowflakes and arctic landscapes, did not help Noa's increasing shivers. Face-to-face with the Polar Parlor itself, the boy had a mental lapse. He stood there for several minutes, unsure of what to do and slowly succumbing to the cold.

Before he could freeze entirely, the front door of the shop opened with a sonorous jingle.

A blonde young woman in a white and purple apron, bearing the name of the titular Parlor, flipped the sign on the door from 'Closed' to 'Open.'

"Hiya, hon'," she smiled radiantly at Noa. "Were you waiting for me to open?"

Noa broke out of his frozen trance, cheeks warming. "Oh, no," he searched his mind for a response but came up blank. "I, um."

"It's blowin' up a storm out there! You look chilled to the bone," she exclaimed, grabbing one of his hands. "Why don't you come in for a cup of Caribou Cocoa? One of our holiday specials."

Startled, Noa pulled his hand back. The young woman looked at him worriedly as he stuffed his hands in his pockets. "Sure," he said quietly. "Thanks."

"Great!" She led him inside the Parlor and the jingling door shut the winter behind them. "Sit anywhere you like, hon'. I don't think many folks will be coming by this early, 'specially on a day so frosty." She got to work on a hot chocolate concoction behind the counter.

Noa sat at a purple table, looking around the shop.

The walls were decorated with the same arctic landscape as the exterior, with silver snowflakes hanging from the ceiling by invisible strings. The counter and napkin holders featured the Parlor's mascot: an anthropomorphic polar bear named Pecan.

The bear was also on the purple apron of the young woman behind the counter, which she wore over a well-fitted white sweater.

Noa felt his cheeks reddening again when she returned with a mug of hot chocolate and marshmallows.

"Ta-dah," she smiled. "One Caribou Cocoa. Enjoy!"

"Thank you," he said, warming his hands on the mug. "How much?"

"Don't worry about it!" she returned to the counter, leaning her back against it. "My treat."

Noa watched her over the fog forming on his glasses from the cocoa's steam.

Is this girl aware that she's working at a Niagara Co. subsidiary? he thought. *Is she an unwitting pawn? A hostage in their web of deceit?*

"How is it?" she asked, interrupting his thoughts. "I added extra marshmallows."

"Oh, um," Noa sampled the hot chocolate. "It's really good. Thank you."

"Aren't you precious! Where're you from, sugar? If you don't mind me asking. You've got a bit of an accent I can't quite distinguish," she said.

Noa took a long sip of the cocoa as he formulated a response. "I'm an exchange student at the local high school. Just started this term."

"No way! That's so neat," she said. "Grand Island Senior High? Where are you visiting from?"

He was in too deep now. "England, but I'm from Sweden originally," he lied, hoping that would explain his ambiguous accent. Most people didn't mention it.

"How fun! I hope you like it here. I'm Elli, by the way," she said with a small curtsy of her apron. "What's your name?"

"Noa," he said, wracking his brain for ways to extract information. "Thank you for the drink. You won't get in trouble?"

Elli giggled. "I appreciate the concern sugar, but no."

"Is this your shop?" Noa asked, as innocently as possible.

"I suppose you could say that," she said, twirling a lock of hair around her fingertip. "The Polar Parlor is my pride and joy."

Interesting, thought Noa. *Perhaps not unwitting after all.* He made an impulsive decision. "Are you hiring?"

Elli considered the question. "I suppose I could use the help," she said after a short pause. "Don't you have school during the day though?" She looked at her watch, "Actually, shouldn't you be at school right now? It's barely 10."

Noa tried to recall the North American education system while staring down the marshmallows floating at the bottom of his mug. "I've got break periods during the day, and I could also work part-time after school."

"You need some earnings on the side, hon'?" Elli's voice softened. "I get that."

Noa stayed quiet.

"Okay," she said, "how about this? Come back after school today and I'll let you know if you can work for me. I just need to check in with my, er," she cleared her throat, "the hiring manager."

"Thank you!" Noa smiled, "I really appreciate it, Elli."

"My pleasure, sugar," she said cheerfully. "Now get your butt to class. I've got work to do."

"Right," he said, finishing the drink and getting up from the table, knowing full well there was no school for him to attend. "See you later, then."

Elli waved him out, and Noa left the Polar Parlor with a mission formulating in his mind.

Instead of going to Grand Island Senior High, he went

down a few streets from the ice cream shop and checked into a hotel.

He dumped the contents of his bag onto the bed and, still under the haze of the morning's adrenaline rush, powered on his work computer. His stomach sank.

A series of emails and secure IMs from his boss popped up on the CSIS virtual chat network as soon as the machine powered on.

Noa reluctantly sat in front of the computer.

[AK | 08:37 AM] Good morning Noa.
[AK | 08:38 AM] Let me know when you are in and have a few mins.
[AK | 09:03 AM] Hi Noa, are you available?
[AK | 09:29 AM] hey came by your desk noticed you're not in yet
[AK | 09:29 AM] going into mtg ping me when you're here
[AK | 10:04 AM] Are you taking the day off? You didn't add anything to the calendar
[AK | 10:05 AM] Are you okay?
[AK | 10:13 AM] noa please respond
[NS | 10:17 AM] Hi yes sorry I'm here
[AK | 10:17 AM] Agent where are you?
[AK | 10:18 AM] What are the charges to your corporate account?
[NS | 10:19 AM] Sorry sorry I forgot to update my status
[NS | 10:19 AM] I am in the US
[AK | 10:20 AM] what
[NS | 10:21 AM] I can reimburse the charges if necessary

[AK | 10:22 AM] forget the charges — why
are you in the US? explain yourself
[NS | 10:23 AM] I pinpointed 2 potential
shell corps of Niagara Co that may have
been established as a base when they
started insider trading
[NS | 10:23 AM] currently investigating
area
[AK | 10:27 AM] I see
[AK | 10:27 AM] I will need to clear this
with the project team. In future, report
all requests for travel & investigation
directly to me. Understood?
[NS | 10:28 AM] yes sir. My apologies
[AK | 10:28 AM] Keep me updated on your
findings. Good work.

Noa sighed with relief. He was expecting something much worse than 'good work,' considering the situation.

Now that he had his employer's blessing, Noa felt reignited with a vigor for his mission.

Locking his laptop in the safe, he grabbed his smokes and a snack from the minibar and left the hotel. The frigid air of the late morning chilled him to the bone, so without much hesitation, he made a detour from his walk towards the river and stopped by a large shopping mall.

He purchased a snug winter jacket and hat using his corporate card, forgetting, again, that Canadian cash was worthless on this side of the border. On his way to the currency exchange kiosk, Noa was sidetracked by the TV displays inside an electronics department store.

The sliding headline read, 'Investment Guru Warren Buffett Strikes Gold on Commodities Market.' A woman with platinum blonde hair was video conferencing the Berkshire-Hathaway CEO during the business segment on CNN.

"—and quite a few experts questioned your large investment in Barrick Gold the other day, isn't that right?" she said, stock tickers zooming by behind her head.

"Indeed Susan, even some of my own staff," Buffet responded with a smug chuckle.

"But then these results! A real *gold mine*, if I may. How big was the gain, if you don't mind my asking?" Susan pried.

"Hm," the old man shrugged, "somewhere in the range of $180 million." The light from the extravagant windows behind him reflected off his golden cufflinks.

"Incredible!" She remarked. "What prompted this investment? Especially considering the recent articles on commodity market volatility. Do you have any advice for prospective traders out there?"

"Well Susan, I try not to let external claims and historical trends influence my decisions," Buffet said confidently. "I like to do my own research."

"It certainly worked out this time," she said. "Now, if anyone has questions for Mr. Buffet, we do have a few spare minutes. You can tweet your questions to @SusanGreeneCNN."

Nearly dropping his new coat, Noa fished out his cellphone from his jeans, typing up a message with lightning speed.

The newscaster held an iPad and scrolled through submitted replies live on the air.

"Oh, here's a good one," she said. "User *@Tetrominoe* writes: 'was it research? Or did you get The Call?'"

The billionaire stiffened.

I knew it, thought Noa.

"Certainly not," said Buffett. "Perhaps I have a guardian angel watching over me, helping me out with my decisions."

"I wish you'd share that angel with us all," the newscaster laughed. "We'll be back in a few short moments with our next top story at 11: Deputy Attorney General Juliette Mercer joins us in the studio to discuss the prosecution of corporate crimes in America."

Noa rolled his eyes and left the storefront.

If Niagara Co.'s insider trading goes beyond company knowledge and into market manipulation, selling information on gold and God knows what else, then they're a lot more powerful than they seem, Noa thought with a frown. *Not to mention unconscionable. As usual, the rich get richer.*

He exchanged his Canadian money for US cash, donned his winter coat and headed back in the direction of the border. Specifically, towards the Polar Parlor.

The mist from the river swirled together with the falling snow, illuminating the Parlor in an otherworldly glow of Christmas lights and desperate rays of sunlight. As he approached, Noa was careful to duck behind trees and cars to avoid detection.

The eagerness to spy on the lone ice cream shop employee trumped Noa's nerves, as he tried to convince himself that she must be in on the Niagara Co.'s scheming somehow. But his apprehensiveness grew as he got closer. The Parlor was bustling with activity.

Upbeat music played from inside the shop's doors and the speakers on the patio. Beyond the frosted windows, Noa could see dozens of people gathered around the pastel-colored tables. Some were dressed in professional attire, others casual.

He caught a glimpse of Elli's bright yellow hair and reflexively pulled the hood of his coat over his head. She was serving treats from a platter, mingling and laughing with the patrons inside.

Noa crept up a little closer, into the alleyway beside the Parlor, to peak in the window. He could make out a banner now, hanging over the counter, held in place with those silver snowflakes on invisible strings. *Run the Rapids?* he squinted. There was something else written below, but he couldn't make it out.

The bells over the door jingled and two people stepped out – a man and a woman. They each held a small paper bag decorated with polar bear stickers and purple gift tissue.

As they headed down Old Falls Street, Noa followed them from behind for a few paces.

"Excuse me," he said once they were a safe distance from the Parlor, "hi, I'm a student at the local high school and I'm writing a piece for our school paper about community events in the area. Do you have a moment?" He smiled politely.

The pair turned around to face him.

"Isn't that nice?" said the woman. She wore an expensive coat over a navy pantsuit. "Do we have time, Rob?"

The man, presumably Rob, checked his Rolex. It glinted in the sun. "Lunch reso's at noon. We have a few minutes, kid. You want to know about the fundraiser?"

Noa glanced back at the Parlor and then withdrew a notebook from his backpack. "That would be great! Any details you can provide would be super helpful."

"Do you need our names?" The woman asked. "I guess it doesn't really matter if it's a school paper. I'm Catherine, and this is my colleague, Robert. We're from the Buffalo Merrill Lynch office."

"He might not know what that is," Rob said to her under his breath. "It's sort of like a bank. We're in finance," he told Noa patronizingly.

Noa suppressed the urge to respond.

"Right, well, anyway, we're here for the *Run the Rapids* fundraiser kick-off," Catherine continued. "It's a half-marathon, I think, around the Niagara river. Both sides of the border, right, Rob?"

Rob nodded, "Yeah, first of its kind. The race isn't till spring but Elli," he pointed to Noa's notebook, "she's the gal that owns this shop, she's hosting a few of these events to raise money and awareness. And they're fun. I brought my daughter to the karaoke one."

"Oh, that *was* fun," Catherine remarked. "This event is adults-only, though. She's handing out samplers of her newest milkshake with an Irish whiskey blend. What did she call it? Tipsy Tundra or something? She's a doll."

"What is the race raising money for?" Noa asked.

"The ALS society," Rob said. "Terrible disease. Apparently, a friend of hers had a father, passed from it a while back. But hey, with all the manpower behind it, I think the charity will get the biggest cheque they've even seen."

"How so?" Noa flipped a page. "Merrill Lynch isn't the only sponsor?"

"Goodness, no!" Catherine exclaimed. "We weren't even interested in this philanthropy when Elli first contacted our PR department some months ago, until she told us the competition is supporting it. Actually, strike that off the record. We love charity work."

"Are there other big firms supporting this event?" Noa asked carefully.

"Kid, other than the runners-in-training, reps from

every Wall Street bank are in there," Rob said. He looked at his watch again, "we need to be heading out, Cath."

"Sorry, one more question," Noa said quickly. "Can you tell me anything about Elli?"

"Shouldn't you interview her yourself, dear?" Catherine said, buttoning up her coat.

"She's, um," Noa stuttered, "she seems really busy today. I'd like to get outside opinions."

Catherine smiled knowingly. "She's so charming, isn't she? Whenever I stop by this area, I say hello. When she's not at the shop, giving out free ice cream to children or hosting some community gathering, she's out and about, helping society."

"My daughter loves Elli," Rob added. "With the amount of free treats she gives out though, I'm always worried I'll see a 'foreclosed' sign next time I'm here."

Noa nodded, jotting his notes down.

"Hope you got what you needed, kid," Rob said. "We need to get going."

"Here, take this," Catherine handed Noa the gift bag.

Alone on the sidewalk, Noa put his notebook away and peered into the bag. There were samplers of various sweets, a pamphlet about the half-marathon and an infographic on ALS. Everything was meticulously designed.

Noa took out a small white chocolate bar, whose wrapper featured Pecan the polar bear and read 'Avalanche Crunch.' He flipped it around. On the back of the wrapper, in elegant cursive text, it said, '*attention to detail; commitment to quality.*'

Noa crumpled the paper bag in his hand and tossed it, along with its contents, into a nearby trash can.

He made his way back to the Polar Parlor and waited for the crowd to disperse from the hidden safety of the alleyway. He lit up a cigarette to stay warm and watched atten-tively as the last of the fundraiser's attendees left the shop. He heard Elli call out goodbyes after them, and then the speakers' music turned off.

Noa glanced at his watch. It was half past noon. He wondered if Elli would be having lunch inside the shop or elsewhere when he was startled by the jingling of the front door. Noa watched, quietly, as Elli exited the Parlor in a puffy winter jacket and earmuffs, locked the door, and headed down Old Falls Street.

He pulled on his hood again and silently followed after her at a distance.

Stopping at a streetlight, Elli dug around in her purse. After a few moments, she pulled out a cellphone and dialed a number, placing the phone under one of the earmuffs on her head.

Noa strained to hear what she was saying.

"Mike? Hey, it's me," she said. "Bassie with you? Kind of a weird situation here I was hoping to run by him. There's this high schooler that wants to work at the Parlor."

The light turned green and Elli continued walking. With more distance between them, Noa couldn't hear the end of the conversation. She hung up about a minute later.

Noa watched as she made her way to the Rainforest Café and went inside. Through the window, he could see her navigating to a table that was occupied by a few young men and women, whom she hugged. They sat down together and ordered lunch, chatting light-heartedly.

What am I doing? Noa thought with a growing frown. *Is this creepy?*

Certain aspects of the Polar Parlor were definitely suspicious. But Elli?

After about half an hour, Elli left the café with one of

the other girls, and Noa followed them to a deteriorating building on the east side of town. He felt his shame manifesting itself deeper when he realized they were at an animal shelter.

Elli and her friend, who evidently also took time off during her workday, spent about two hours with the neglected animals inside. Noa peeked in a few times to see Elli either feeding a one-eyed cat or washing an old dog.

He leaned against the wall and groaned.

Finally, Elli left the shelter, waving goodbye to her friend. She was in a hurry.

As she broke into a light jog, Noa struggled to keep up with her. Back at the Parlor, Elli quickly unlocked the entrance and rushed inside, bells signaling her arrival.

Out of breath, Noa returned to his post by the side window of the shop. He was tired and hungry but determined to see this spy mission through.

At around 3:30 in the afternoon, a large white van pulled up to the front of the Parlor. Noa straightened up with anticipation. The driver of the van emerged, opening the sliding doors for the passengers

Noa's enthusiasm deflated.

A group of 10 or so elderly women exited the van, as Elli excitedly held the Polar Parlor's door open with an extended arm and welcomed them inside with cheerful greetings. She had changed into an exercise outfit, resembling that of a 70s yoga instructor.

Dejected, Noa looked through the corner of the window. The Parlor's interior had been transformed – tables and chairs pushed aside to the walls, revealing a wide-open space with a bright and pleasant atmosphere. A handmade disco ball twirled on an invisible string alongside the ceiling's snowflakes.

He watched as Elli removed the seniors' coats and welcomed each of them individually with a warm smile, before skipping to the front of the shop and adjusting a delicate headset.

"Alrighty, ladies!" he heard her say through the speakers by the window. "Are y'all ready to move?! Time for the warm up!"

The Weather Girls' *It's Raining Men* started to play, and Noa slumped down against the brick wall of the Parlor.

A few songs later, the cold and hunger got the better of him, and he gave up. To the tune of *Girls Just Want to Have Fun*, Noa snuck out of the alley and wandered into a nearby Starbucks.

He sat there until sundown, sulking over cups of coffee and an underwhelming sandwich, staring at the pages of his notebook. All he had written down from his conversation with the two Merrill Lynch employees was, *why Wall St. execs travel to Niagara???* And, *is run the rapids real?* Beside which he had later written 'yes,' after a quick Google search.

Further down the page, Noa had written that slogan: *Attention to detail; commitment to quality.* Beside it, he wrote, *Niagara Co. & Polar Parlor – why?* Then, in bold, ***money laundering???***

In the center of the page, the word 'Elli' was circled multiple times. Next to it, the question 'in on it?' was underlined twice. *Yes* and *no* floated around the centerpiece, both crossed out and re-written.

Noa sighed, resting his head on the notebook.

If the Polar Parlor was a front, a subsidiary, of the Niagara Co., then it must be engaging in illegal activity. If Elli owns the Polar Parlor, she too must be engaging in illegal activity. Noa certainly didn't expect field agent work to be easy, but he felt betrayed by his instincts.

As the afterwork rush began in the Starbucks, Noa hastily packed up to avoid the crowd. Before he left, he saw a brief headline of the breaking news on the TV in the coffee shop's corner. *Two bodies discovered in isolated district of Venetian island – suspected Mafia activity.*

Back at the Polar Parlor, Noa knocked on the front door hesitantly.

Elli swung it open, "Hi, sugar! No need to knock, we're open 'til ten on Fridays." She beckoned him inside. "Don't tell me. Noa, right?"

The boy nodded, stepping inside. "Sorry if I'm late," he said.

"No trouble at all," Elli sat at a rosy pink table and motioned for Noa to join her. "Winter evenings are light on customers. Come, come. How was school?"

Noa sat across from her, removing his coat and backpack. "It was fine," he said, studying the glittering snowflake pattern on the tabletop. "Uneventful."

From his periphery, he felt Elli's sea-green eyes studying him closely.

"Did you have dinner already?" she asked. "I don't have much food here, but I can make us some tea and snacks."

"I'm okay," he started, but Elli was already getting up.

"It'll just take a sec," she said with a smile. "Milk in your tea? Sugar?"

Noa fidgeted with his sweater sleeve. "Just some milk, please."

"You got it!" she said, sliding behind the counter.

While Elli prepared the drinks, humming a tune to herself, Noa looked around the Parlor. Multi-colored lights adorned the windowpanes, glowing faintly against the darkness of the cold outdoors. A community board hung on the western wall, with a large events calendar.

Elli returned with two mugs and a platter of cookies, setting them down on the table. "Order up!"

"Thank you," he said, warming himself up with the milk tea.

"My pleasure, hon'," She sat down again, breaking off a cookie piece for herself. "So, just wondering, why were you following me around all day?"

Noa choked on the tea, some of it coming back up through his nose. "I— what?" He coughed, covering his face with a napkin.

Elli took a small bite of the cookie, watching him silently.

Noa swallowed nervously. "I'm sorry, I just—" He hesitated. What could he say?

"You can be honest with me," she said softly. "What's really going on?"

Noa sniffed, gazing down at his tea. *She's worried about me,* he thought. *I can work with that.*

"The truth is," he said quietly, "I don't want to go home."

"Home," Elli repeated. "You mean, back abroad?"

Noa nodded, maintaining eye-contact with the liquid instead. "I went on exchange to get away from my, um," he faltered. "My family. But now that I'm here, school doesn't really matter to me."

Elli bit her lip. "And you want to make some money so you can stay here, rather than return to your folks?"

"I would rather do anything than return," he said, surprised by the ease with which he crafted this story. "The high school is useless. I need to start making some savings."

Elli held up her mug. "That settles it, then! You're hired, sugar."

Noa looked up in surprise, "Really?"

"Really!" She smiled, "But I don't approve of skipping classes. You can work for me part-time, and on the weekends. What's the going rate these days? How about $30 an hour?"

He gaped at her. This side job would add a solid bonus to his regular salary. "Are you sure?"

"Sure, I'm sure," she giggled. "Now come on, I'll show you the ropes."

Over the next few hours, Elli showed Noa the ins and outs of ice cream scooping, cash registering, and basic customer service. A few people came in throughout the evening, but for the most part, business was slow.

Noa was sweeping the floors when he stopped by the 'Staff Only' door.

"I noticed there were two floors," he said. "What's above the shop? An apartment?"

"Oh, no," Elli paused her task of arranging a chocolate display. "That's the office. No need for you to worry about that, hon'. It's just where we plan the budgets and events and whatnot. Boring stuff," she winked.

Noa made an effort to conceal his intrigue. "There are other employees besides us?"

"Sure! Well, kind of," she said, bringing a finger to her chin. "There's that hiring manager I mentioned. And, you see, the office space is shared between the Polar Parlor and a winery on Pine Street, so the guys from there use it too. Sometimes they'll help me out here."

Bella Luna Winery, if Noa recalled correctly. The second subsidiary he considered.

"You're usually on your own?" he asked.

"I make do," Elli said proudly. "But I will admit, it'll be nice to have someone here to watch over the shop while I'm out or running errands."

Noa nodded absentmindedly. He wasn't sure how long his superiors would allow this 'investigation' to continue, especially while he was going nowhere in a hurry.

Once the Parlor's clock chimed ten, Elli flipped the 'Open' sign to 'Closed.'

"Good work today, 'hon! See you tomorrow?" she said, making her way back to the counter.

"Of course," said Noa. "Thanks again."

He grabbed his coat and backpack from the table in the corner of the shop, when the jingling bells rang out once more.

He turned to see a man in a large brown trench coat enter the Parlor, pulling two thick suitcases behind him. He held the door open and was soon followed by a second man, younger and strikingly handsome, in a sleek black coat and even blacker hair.

"Elli!" Exclaimed the one in the trench coat. *"Bon-gee-or-noh!"*

"Mikey!" Elli ran over to give him a hug. "I wasn't expecting you guys this early. How are ya?"

"I'm pooped," Mike said. "Lucy went home already, but we just wanted to drop these off," he motioned to the luggage. "I'll take care of 'em."

"Bassie workin' you like a dog?" she asked, nudging the second man playfully with her elbow.

He smiled briefly at Elli, "I do no such thing. And don't call me that." He removed his coat and turned to face Noa. "Who is this?"

Noa, standing sheepishly in the corner holding his

belongings, suddenly felt paralyzed by the question. He opened his mouth to speak but no sound emerged.

"That's my newest employee," Elli said. "The one I called about, remember?"

"I see," the man said as he took a few steps toward the boy.

Noa's blood ran cold, though he wasn't sure why. This must be the so-called 'hiring manager' Elli mentioned, but there was such an intensity about his presence that Noa felt unable to move.

The man stopped about two feet away from him. He towered over Noa.

"What's your name?" he asked in a smooth voice. He looked relatively young, but everything about him was intimidating somehow. His eyes, piercing icy blue, would not break contact with Noa's own.

"...It's Noa," he finally managed to stammer out.

"Noa," the man echoed. He held out his right hand, and Noa could not help but admire the craftsmanship of his suit.

The boy shook his hand, startled by the firm grip.

"Nice to meet you, Noa," the man said. "Sebastian Nové."

EIGHT

NIAGARA CO

- Niagara Falls. February 8, 2014 -

The moment Noa's head hit the hotel pillow that Friday night, he was out cold. The adrenaline surge of boarding a train and crossing the border, staking out an (alleged) mafia location and interacting with an almost record number of strangers drained his mental energy to zero.

At dawn, the gentle light of the winter sun peeking through window of his room awakened him, hours before the alarm. Noa sat up with a start as the events of the previous day washed over.

The Polar Parlor and its suspicious lack of income. Elli and her suspicious generosity. Mike and those suspicious suitcases. And most suspicious of them all, Sebastian the *hiring manager*.

Noa balled the thick hotel comforter in his fists. The Parlor was definitely hiding *something*, but he needed evidence.

Grabbing his glasses, he looked at the bedside clock. 7:30 AM. The Polar Parlor opened at 10:00, and Elli wasn't expecting him until 10:30. Determined to succeed this time, Noa got to work on a new plan.

Retrieving his computer from the safe, he also fished out the little 11-marked cube from his backpack and a few cables. With a paper cup of substandard hotel coffee and a few candy bars pilfered from the mini-fridge, Noa sat on the bed, hunched over the laptop in concentration, creating a bite-sized, undetectable program.

At about five to 10:00, he unplugged the cube from the computer, switching its cable for a mobile-compatible one and connected it to his cellphone. The cube powered on once more, glowing with a faint white light.

Noa reset the phone anxiously, unsure if his idea would work.

Once it restarted, he navigated to the app he needed and tested the function, monitoring his laptop screen for any changes. His eyes twinkled with pride. It worked.

The Parlor's owner turned behind the counter to face the door when its jingling bells announced Noa's arrival. She crossed her arms in mock annoyance.

"You're late, mister. And on your first official day of work!"

"I know, I'm so sorry," Noa said quickly. "I got lost on the way here," he lied. "It won't happen again!"

In reality, right before leaving the hotel, Noa had realized that he ran out of clothes and had to spend corporate money on his wardrobe yet again.

"It better not," Elli chastised playfully. "But I'll let you off with a warning this time, since you're new and all."

Noa nodded, changing out of his jacket and donning a

Polar Parlor apron that Elli prepared for him. He placed his backpack behind the counter, out of sight. He almost asked if he could leave it in the upstairs office, but considering the contents of his laptop, which was inside the bag, decided not to risk it.

The morning passed uneventfully.

Elli showed Noa a few specialty recipes and he helped her prepare a custom-made ice cream cake for a regular customer. Despite the lack of progress on his investigation, he selfishly enjoyed Elli's company. Some part of him hoped he was wrong about her accomplice status.

"Did you always want to open an ice cream shop?" Noa asked, half probing, half genuinely curious.

Elli placed the finished cake into a purple and white box, tying it with a silver bow. "That's a good question, sugar. I've always wanted to have my own business. Did I think in a million years I'd end up here when I was little? Probably not."

Noa caught a brief glimpse of her expression. "What's wrong?"

The flash of sorrow was gone as quickly as it had appeared. She smiled, "Nothing! You know what they say, hon'. Play the cards you're dealt, right?" She slid the cake into the freezer.

He considered asking what cards she had been dealt to end up here but thought better of it. Instead, he just nodded, putting away the baking utensils.

Elli checked her watch, heading over to the 'Staff Only' door. "Listen hon', I have to prepare some budget reports today. Quarter end, ugh," she made a face. "Think you can hold down the fort for a couple hours?"

Noa prayed his inquisitiveness didn't show on his face.

"Sure thing," he said, a tad too quickly. "Will you be in the office upstairs; in case I need you?"

Hand on the door handle, Elli hesitated. "Of course, but I might be on the phone with our other partners." She took out her cellphone, "How about I give you my number and if you have any urgent questions, you can shoot me a text?"

Noa suppressed a triumphant grin. "Sure!"

They exchanged phone numbers and Elli's cell pinged with a text notification.

"I texted you from mine," said Noa.

"Oh, my goodness," she squealed at her screen, "that's too precious! Where did you get these stickers? Is that a polar bear? It looks just like Pecan!"

"It's this new app from Japan," he said as convincingly as possible. "They have all sorts of stickers. If you tap on the one I sent you, you can download them too."

"Done!" Elli busily scrolled through a catalog of adorable animals. "My friends will love this. Oh, a puppy!"

Noa slid his phone back into his pocket with a satisfied smile.

Elli cleared her throat, "Okay, so, text me if anything. I should be done in a couple hours, max! I'm sure you'll be fine, sugar." She disappeared behind the 'Staff Only' door with a wave.

After some time had passed, when he was sure the girl was not returning, Noa ducked under the counter and pulled his laptop out from his bag.

His program from the morning was still running. He refreshed it, watching as a map of Niagara Falls populated the screen. This time, instead of one red blip on the map, there were two. Both blinking intermittently at the intersection of 1st and Old Falls St. The Polar Parlor.

Noa allowed himself a celebratory fist pump. Then he looked around to make sure no one was watching.

He turned off his own cellphone, so that only one blip hovered over the Parlor on the map. He labeled it with an "E" and modified the color to pink.

The bells of the front door jingled, and Noa quickly shut the laptop, pushing it aside.

A man and a little girl entered the Parlor. She raced to the counter excitedly, but her enthusiasm faded into a frown as she approached.

"You're not Elli," she said accusingly.

"Um, no," Noa agreed. "Elli's not here right now."

"Where is Elli?!" The girl demanded, stomping her foot.

The man, presumably her father, came up behind her. "Sorry about this. Lizzie, manners."

She shook her head, frustrated. "I want Elli!"

"She's busy, but I can help you out," Noa said gently. "I'm new."

"Elli makes the best cakes," the girl said spitefully.

"We placed an order," her father said. "Lizzie only likes Polar Parlor treats, so we always come here."

"You're just in time," Noa said as he got the cake from the freezer. "Elli and I just finished it a little while ago." He presented the wrapped-up box to Lizzie, "Is this your cake?"

The stared at the sparkly packaging, entranced. "Yes!"

"I didn't know Elli was hiring," the man said, paying for the cake. "It's nice that she'll have some help. She's always doing everything on her own. All those events and running the shop."

Noa nodded. "You two are regulars?"

"I love Elli!" The girl named Lizzie shouted. "She gives me chocolates!"

"Yes," the man said, "she's always giving Lizzie some goodie for free. We really ought not to accept it! Well, when you see Elli, tell her Richard and Lizzie say 'hi.'"

He took the cake and thanked Noa, leading his daughter out by the hand.

Once they left, Noa opened his laptop again with the goal of researching Niagara Co. However, out of sheer curiosity, he first decided to refresh the map.

His eyes widened.

Elli's pink marker was gone from the intersection of 1st and Old Falls.

Noa panicked. Did she turn off her phone? Did she realize that he tricked her into installing a GPS tracker?

He entered a command prompt to zoom out and subsequently sighed with relief. The 'E' was still on the map, but now it was at a new location. Pine Avenue and 6th Street.

Pine Avenue? Why did that sound familiar? He opened a new tab and searched the intersection.

"Bella Luna Winery," he muttered under his breath. He flipped back to the map. When did Elli leave? And from where? She didn't use the front entrance.

Noa furrowed his brows. He looked up to the hooks at the front of the Parlor, where his brand-new winter jacket hung beside Elli's puffy one. Did she walk all the way to the Little Italy district in the freezing cold without a coat?

He refreshed the map again. The pink blip was moving! He refreshed the screen repeatedly to track its signal.

From the Bella Luna, Elli's pink marker made its way west along Pine, then south along Main Street. Noa could not comprehend what he was seeing. The glowing dot continued west towards the Niagara River.

But the blip didn't stop at the riverbank. It continued

blinking, as if it was mocking him, over the pixelated blues of the Hell's Half Acre. As if Elli was walking on water.

Noa concluded that it must be broken as he watched Elli's digital representation on the screen. He looked up at the ceiling. Was she really out?

He shut the laptop, stashed it in a drawer, and opened the 'Staff Only' door.

There was nothing particularly interesting inside – just an employee storage area and a bathroom, with some extra supplies on wooden shelves and decorations for the shop. He glanced at the stairway leading to the second floor. There was also an elevator next to the staircase with just two buttons: 1st and 2nd floor.

He thought this was odd for a two-story building, but then again, the stairway was tall, and at least it was accessible. He thought back to the loud man, Mike, from the night before, carrying two large suitcases. And Elli said she got boxes of supplies she took upstairs sometimes.

Apprehensively, he climbed the stairs.

Noa stopped at the ornate oak door at the top. He pressed his ear against it. Nothing.

He knocked. "Elli? Are you there?"

No response. He tried the handle, but it was locked. Of course.

So how did she leave? Noa reluctantly descended the stairs again and took up his post at the counter. He opened his computer and refreshed the map in time to see the pink blip a mere block away from the Polar Parlor.

With a quiet gasp, he closed the laptop and hid it in his backpack, returning it to its hiding spot beneath the counter. He busied himself with the cookie display, keeping an eye on the entrance. No one entered.

A little while later, Elli emerged from the 'Staff Only' only door.

"Hi, sugar!" She grabbed a cookie from the platter he was arranging. "How'd it go? Anyone give you trouble?"

"All good," he said. "Lizzie and Richard came for their cake. They give their regards."

"Lovely!" Elli gave him a thumbs up. "I knew you could handle it."

"How was your work?" Noa asked, eyeing her out of his periphery.

She was dressed the same as before she left – a dark green knit sweater dress under a Polar Parlor apron. Her boots showed no sign of slush or snow residue and her face didn't betray any rosy signs of sudden entry into the warmth.

Elli shrugged, "All good on my end too. Crossed all the i's, dotted all the t's. Now that that's done though, how about we go get some lunch?"

Noa knew he couldn't possibly pry without arousing suspicion, so he agreed.

The rest of the day, lunch inclusive, passed without incident. Elli didn't leave the Parlor until closing, after which Noa felt creepy checking her location.

On his way back to the hotel, Noa walked along Pine Avenue. He stopped at Pine and 6th, in front of the Bella Luna winery. It was closed.

He circled the perimeter of the building, looking for some hidden entrance. He gave up relatively quickly though, as the evening cold settled over the hushed streets, carrying frozen mist off the Falls on blistery winds.

As he was leaving, he thought he saw a slender woman in a dark hood exiting the Bella Luna from a side door, but as he turned back, she was gone.

Noa knew he was on the right track. Frustrated by the lack of evidence, his determination grew together with his suspicion.

- Niagara Falls. February 12, 2014 -

Four days came and went. Elli taught Noa how to restock the inventory, how to blend milkshakes, how to decorate cakes, how to use the cash register and card machines, and how to deal with unruly customers.

In some fleeting moments, Noa would forget about his case entirely. Then he would remember, and the irritating lack of progress would sour his mood.

On Monday, Elli held a fundraiser in the Parlor, raising well over ten thousand dollars for a local children's hospital. There was a karaoke contest; the winners would get a year's supply of ice cream.

Noa was in charge of collecting and safekeeping the donations and all of it did indeed, to his relief, go to the hospital.

By Wednesday, Noa felt fairly settled into his fake new job. He enjoyed spending time with Elli, who frequently took him out for meals and showed him around the area. He hadn't seen any more of that man with the suitcases or the strange woman from the Bella Luna, and he'd mostly forgotten the incident.

Occasionally a man in a white suit would stop by, heading straight to the 'Staff Only' door. He once introduced himself to Noa as Nick, but never mentioned his position in the Parlor. As for the threatening 'hiring manager,' Noa hadn't seen him again either.

Wednesday afternoon, Elli received a call on her cell

while her and Noa were setting up Valentine's Day decorations.

"Hello?" She held the phone to her ear and stayed silent for a while. "Alrighty. I'm coming now." She hung up and turned to Noa, "Sorry hon', emergency meeting! I'll be back in a jiffy. You'll be okay on your own, right?"

Noa nodded, curiosity piquing. "Of course."

"If you need me," she paused. "Um, don't need me. I'll see you soon!" With that, Elli disappeared behind the 'Staff Only' door. It closed gently behind her.

Noa finished hanging up the red heart decorations and went behind counter, pondering what to do. He hadn't brought his backpack or laptop today, having slept in and leaving his hotel room in a hurry.

The bells of the front door chimed a few minutes later, and a woman entered the Parlor.

"Hi," she said, approaching the counter.

"Hello," Noa straightened up. "How can I help you?"

"Do you sell gift cards?" she asked. "My friend loves this place. I want to give her a gift card as a present."

"Um, I'm not sure actually," Noa said, taking out his cellphone. "I'm new here, but I can ask my manager if you'll just give me a moment. I need to call her."

The woman sighed. "I'm kind of in a hurry."

Noa glanced back at the employee door. "Um, okay. I can go look for her. Sorry, just hang on a few minutes."

He went behind the 'Staff Only' door and darted up the stairs to the office.

"Elli?" He knocked gently. "There's a lady here asking about gift cards. Do we have those?"

No response. He tried the door, but it was locked, as usual.

Where did she go now?

Confused, he went back down the stairs, past the elevator, and into the storage room. He looked in a few of the boxes and along the shelves, hoping to find gift cards there.

From beyond the employee door, he heard the woman shout, "I'm leaving!" and then the jingling of the door.

Noa frowned, reaching on his tiptoes for an upper shelf. It looked empty, but he also couldn't see from his height. He felt along the shelf until his fingers brushed over something card-like. He tried to pull at it, but it wouldn't budge. Straining to see and in an effort to lift himself up, he pressed down.

He heard a *click*.

His head spun around to the source of the noise. The elevator.

Noa bolted back to the lift, which was standing open and waiting on the ground floor.

He all but trembled with bewilderment. The space beneath the numbered button panel had slid open, revealing a hidden set of accessible floors, numbered -1 to -15. -13 was missing.

Without thinking, Noa stepped into the elevator. He tried to steady his breathing, wrapping his head around the notion that the Polar Parlor was in fact a cover up.

Noa pulled out his cellphone and turned on the flash. He shined it over the numbered buttons. Three in particular seemed more worn than the rest: -1, -6, and -14. Riding the thrill of his finding, he started with the closest and descended to the first basement floor.

The elevator doors closed and re-opened without a sound. Noa stepped out into a hallway. The walls were placarded with heavy-duty metal and the ceiling lights shone with a bright luminescent glow.

"Whoa." Noa marveled at the surroundings. *This hall must extend at least 100 feet!*

Large doors lined the walls, and Noa carefully checked them one by one. They were all locked tight. Dejected, he went back to the elevator and descended further to the sixth.

As soon as the elevator opened again, Noa could hear people talking. He recognized one of the voices and immediately stepped out. This hall was not as long and not as threatening, ending with two wooden doors from behind which the voices emerged.

Noa crept along the wall quietly, placing one foot in front of the other with the softness of a cat. As he approached the wooden doors, he could hear the voices more clearly. The one he recognized initially was Sebastian's, the hiring manager from a few days back.

He realized another was Elli's. A few others spoke as well. They were discussing something.

He pressed his ear up against the door carefully, trying to tune into the conversation. He heard Sebastian speaking, although in a different tone than the one he used during their brief encounter.

"...Mala del Brenta is out, we can't rely on them anymore. But it's a chance to expand into the European stock market."

"Would we need liaisons in European cities?"

"Can we trust them?"

"What wrong with the NASDAQ and New York, Boss?"

Noa was in awe. *This is it,* he thought. *It's definitely them.*

"Hang on a sec, guys. I really need to take a piss."

Before Noa had a chance to back away, the left door swung open with a mighty force and collided with his head.

Stumbling back, the last thing he heard was, "What the fuck?" before he blacked out.

———

Nick nearly tripped over the fallen lump of a boy before his feet.

"What the fuck?" He stepped over the body. "What's he doing here?"

Elli jumped up, "That's Noa!" She hurried over to the door, crouching down, "Oh no. Oh dear. Noa? Hon'?" She rubbed his back, "Anyone home?"

Nick crouched down too, "I think I knocked him out good."

Getting up from his seat, Sebastian walked over to them as well. "Elli, how did he get here? Did you show him how to access the lift?"

"No, no!" Elli raised her hands, proclaiming her innocence. "I would never. He probably tried to find me in the back for whatever reason, poor boy. Maybe he found the switch by accident."

"Quite an accident," Sebastian remarked.

Nick turned Noa over, so he was lying on his back. "Ouch, that'll be a nice shiner in the morning."

"Do you think he'll be okay?" Elli bit her lip worriedly.

Mike also made his way to the door, Lucy opting to stay behind. He kneeled by Noa. "I think it'll just be a bruise. Unless Nick gave him a concussion."

Elli gasped, "Don't say that!"

"What should we do, Boss?" Mike asked.

Sebastian leaned against the doorframe. "Search him."

Now it was Lucy's turn to join the crowd examine the young intruder. She searched his clothes for anything removable in silence while the others waited.

On the floor beside her, she placed a carton of cigarettes, a cellphone, a wallet, a Polar Parlor napkin, and a pack of gum.

"That's all," Lucy said, getting up.

"Oh my god," Elli exclaimed, picking up the cigarettes. "He smokes! How awful." She tossed them into the meeting room's trashcan. "He'll die young!"

Nick coughed, "You never cared that I smoke."

"I don't care if *you* die." Elli retorted.

Sebastian intercepted, raising his hand. "Pass me his phone."

Lucy handed him the phone, and Sebastian examined it. The cell didn't have a passcode and he browsed through the contents.

"So?" Elli asked.

"Doesn't appear to be a threat," Sebastian started to say.

"I told you!" Elli patted the top of Noa's unconscious head. "He's a good boy. I reckon he got down here by accident, no doubt about it."

"But what do we do now?" Mike looked back to the meeting room. "He probably heard something."

Nick scoffed. "Please. You think this kid understands words like 'stock market?'"

"Considering you didn't understand them a year ago, maybe you've got a point." Elli said.

"What, you're actually agreeing with me?" Nick spat.

Sebastian sighed, handing the cellphone to Lucy. "Can you put everything back, Luce?"

"Except the cancer sticks!" Elli interjected.

Lucy nodded, returning Noa's belongings to his pockets. She then lifted his unconscious body with ease.

"What should we do with him, chief?" Nick asked. "Just leave him in the Parlor?"

"No," Sebastian said. "Take him to my office. I'd like to have a talk with him when he wakes up."

Elli frowned. "You're not going fire him, are you, Bassie?"

Sebastian shook his head once, "I just want to see how much he heard."

She looked down, "And if he heard a lot? What then?"

"As Nick said, I doubt he understood much." He looked to the motionless form in Lucy's arms. "But if I determine him to be a threat, then. Well, we'll see."

"He's just a child, though!"

"That's enough, Elli." Sebastian started towards the elevator. "Lucy, my office."

"What about the meeting, Boss?" Mike asked.

"We'll resume tomorrow." With that, Sebastian and Lucy, with Noa in her arms, took the elevator down to the 14th floor.

Elli, Mike and Nick remained near the meeting room.

"Unbelievable," Elli huffed, "how can he be so suspicious of a child?"

"You have to admit El', it's weird that he found his way down here," Mike said, sitting against the wall. "And on top of figuring out the elevator, he figured out which floor we're on."

"That's not exactly hard to figure out! He probably just tried each floor until he heard us," she said adamantly. "You don't trust him either?"

Mike shrugged, "I don't know him. He seems innocent enough."

Elli ran a hand through her hair. "I hope so."

"Who knows?" Mike said, "maybe the kid will join our team?"

"Ha, good one." Nick laughed.

NINE

ELISE "ELLI" RENÉ

- Chicago, Illinois. April 2010 -

It was early Spring when Sebastian had docked *Aurora II* in the Windy City's pier. He didn't stay on shore for long, though.

Rumors had been spreading among his Illinois contacts, and across the Great Lakes, of an exceptionally talented gambler, known in the underground only as The Businessman.

This mysterious figure was supposedly operating on one of the Lake Michigan riverboat casinos at the time, so Sebastian decided to see for himself. He had a vested interest.

Inside, his attention was immediately drawn to a college-aged girl, an entanglement of blonde curls and an outfit of bright colors, barely old enough to step foot in a casino. A small crowd was gathering around her.

"Hit me," she cooed, pointing to the green fuzzy table.

Sebastian inched closer. The pit boss barely noticed him, too distracted by the Blackjack table. His face was wound up in a grimace.

The dealer flipped over a Queen, bringing her face-up card total to 19. Her audience murmured. Sebastian was close enough now to see the stack of chips beside the girl's elbows.

She smiled a beautiful smile at the dealer. "Hit me, sugar."

The onlookers gasped; some voiced their concern. The rest froze with anticipation. The dealer's forehead was sweating under the fluorescent lamplight. He flipped the next card.

Sebastian recoiled from the noise as the crowd erupted in cheers. A two of spades.

"Blackjack," the dealer said with gritted teeth. "Again."

"Yippee!" The girl hugged the chips to her chest, some of them spilling over the table. She glanced back for a second and, noting the reddeningly mad face of the casino employee watching her, scooted off the stool.

"That's it for today, missy?" asked one of her onlookers.

The girl finished collecting her chips. "Hm. I think I'll try my luck at Texas Hold'em," she said invitingly. "If anyone wants to join me?"

With a theatrical twirl, she made her way to the poker tables. Sebastian followed as the girl sat down at a table of businessmen. Investment bankers, brokers, traders and the like, he figured.

They sized her up, exchanging a few chuckles and crude comments. While the dealer shuffled the deck, the girl cleared her throat.

"You seem like fine gentlemen," she said, a slight southern accent peeking its way out among her words. "How about we make this game a bit more fun?"

The men eyed her, some lecherously.

"What do you have in mind?" asked one.

"I studied business, you see," she said, coiling a lock of golden hair around her finger. "I want to get some investing experience. How about, if I win," she tilted her head to the side, exposing the curve of her neckline, "you gentlemen invest $10,000 each into my portfolio."

"And if one of us wins?" another responded, gaze glued to her chest as she leaned forward on the poker table.

She twirled the Big Blind chip. "I reckon I'll go on a date with the winner, and give $10,000 to each of you, how about that?"

With the terms agreed upon, the pot opened, and the dealer began to distribute the cards.

"Mind if I join?" Sebastian asked, taking a seat across from the girl. Before she could respond, the dealer handed him two cards.

The girl studied him before looking at her own hand. "Not at all, sugar."

After about an hour, three of the players had dropped out. The girl, Sebastian, and two other businessmen remained in the game.

Sebastian was impressed. He figured she must have been card counting at the Blackjack tables, but the source of her consistency in poker skill was harder to discern. Everyone studied their cards as the dealer called River and added a fifth card face-up to the table.

"Fold," Sebastian said. Not worth the risk. He watched the girl, who was in turn watching the two others.

One of the men called all-in. The girl and the second man called his raise.

Upon the reveal, the two remaining businessmen were out. Only the girl and Sebastian remained in the game.

"You have to win this, man," the latest player said to Sebastian. "I can't just give this chick 10K to invest."

Sebastian pushed his ante into the pot. "Ah, my apologies. Since I joined late, I figured I was not part of your bargain with the young lady." He turned to the man, "It would appear the five of you already owe her your investments. Unless you are dishonorable players."

The men grumbled in outrage, but, annoyed at being called out, followed through with the deal. They each wrote a cheque for $10,000, for the girl to invest as she pleased. Though she did promise to achieve favorable returns for them.

As the others left, the girl smiled. "I like you," she said, tossing her ante into the pot. "What's your name?"

"Sebastian Nové," he said. The dealer distributed their cards. "And yourself?"

"Elli." She peaked at her cards. "Just Elli."

Sebastian looked at his cards as well. "Nice to meet you, 'Just Elli.' Or should I say *Businessman?* I've heard a lot about you."

Elli raised a brow. "I figured you weren't some ordinary type, sugar. If you know that name, then you're either with the mafia or the feds, and I'm really hoping it's the former."

The dealer called Flop and flipped three cards face up on the table. A ten of hearts, a ten of clubs and a four of spades. Wordlessly, Sebastian watched her, chin resting on the palm of his hand.

"How much *do* you know?" She asked, tracing the outline of her cards.

"Just the rumors," he said casually. "For example, those vulgar men feel as though they've been robbed of $50,000. But that's not the case at all, is it? In fact, based on your historical returns, you're quite the successful investor."

Elli smirked proudly. "I'm hoping they'll come around."

Sebastian's own two cards were lying face down on the

table. He tapped the table twice, for check. "Would you be open to making a deal of our own, Ms. Businessman?"

She checked as well, signaling the end of the turn. "I'm all ears."

The dealer called Turn and added a Jack of hearts to the table. Neither of the players reacted.

"If I win, you'll come work for me," Sebastian said, checking again.

"Interesting," Elli replied, checking as well. "You're offering me a job? No background check or anything?" She tapped her fingers on the tabletop. "And if I win?"

"I'll cut you a cheque for $1,000,000," he said.

"Just like that?" Elli said. "Alright Bassie, you've got a deal."

Sebastian blinked. "Bassie?" he repeated.

"You don't like it?" she asked.

"No," he said. "Never say that again."

Elli giggled as the dealer added the final card to the table, calling River. An Ace of hearts.

"All in," Sebastian said, pushing every chip in front of him to the center of the table.

Elli hesitated. She searched Sebastian's eyes. "What've you lived through?"

"Beg your pardon?" Sebastian asked.

"I can't seem to read your face at all," she said, crestfallen. "You can't be much older than me, and yet your eyes look so haunted."

"Does that mean the Businessman folds?"

Elli scoffed. "Nice try, Bassie. Call." She pushed all her chips into the pot.

"Reveal," the dealer said.

"Four of a kind," Elli said, revealing two more tens.

Sebastian flipped over a King and Queen of hearts.

"Royal flush," she breathed. "Lucky duck."

"You knew I would win," Sebastian said. "You paused before matching my bet. Why did you do it?"

"I could use a job," Elli shrugged. "Now, as my new colleague, will you divulge how you *really* know me?"

Sebastian smiled. "It would appear you can read my face after all." He stood from the table, "Shall we?"

"Lead the way, Bassie!"

The truth is, while Sebastian had first met Elli in Chicago, this was not the first time he had seen her. Nor was her underground fame as the Businessman the reason for his interest. To understand that, we need to go back.

- South Carolina. Summer 1988 -

Elise René was born the eldest of three siblings to a poor family in a small Southern town called White Rock.

White Rock had a population of about 400 and featured a post office, a golf course, a retirement home, and about ten churches of various denominations. The town's only advantageous feature was its proximity to Lake Murray, a few miles south.

The René's lived in a humble home on the East side of town. Elise shared a tiny bedroom with her brother and sister, which had a window looking out onto the Hopewell Cemetery.

Mr. René worked at the local automotive shop. He was a kind and quiet man, working long hours to support his family. His high school sweetheart, Mrs. René, raised the children until they were old enough to attend school, after which she took a part-time job at the old folks' home.

School was tedious and days were dull for the bright-eyed, quick-witted Elise. Once, on a particularly rebellious whim, the young girl followed her mother to the retirement home instead of Spring Hill Elementary.

By the time Mrs. René had realized that her daughter played hooky and tagged along, she could not separate her from the seniors. Nor could Elise's new friends let her go. She delighted them with her infectious joy, and likewise the girl was enthralled by their tales of times gone by.

Her mother made a deal: if her teachers allowed it, Elise could join her twice a week. The girl did that, of course, and also came by on weekends.

She quickly befriended two elderly war veterans named Max and Louie, who spent almost all of their time playing cards by the light of the window. Elise watched with interest as they argued about cheating and exchanged pista-chios or stamps after every game.

After observing a few games, Elise asked if she could play. At the tender age of ten, Elise learned how to play community card poker.

By summer break, she mastered the popular card games. Blackjack, Texas Hold'em, 5-card draw, Baccarat. By her 11th birthday, Max and Louie could not beat her.

Elise breezed through her classes, earning the highest arithmetic scores in the history of White Rock. She enrolled in high school early, skipping eighth grade.

During the day, Elise would studiously attend her classes at Grace Point High, maintaining a stellar GPA and a resume filled with various extracurriculars. With the setting of the sun, she would shed her school uniform, retrieve her treasured white bicycle, and make the 40-minute journey down to Yacht Cove.

It wasn't the largest marina in South Carolina by far, but a fair number of retirees with deep pockets came by to sail and relax on Lake Murray. A perfect training ground for Elise.

Wearing clothes that she'd borrowed from her older friends to look more mature, Elise would approach unsuspecting pensioners with a radiant smile and silver briefcase. It was a parting gift from her dear friend Max. He passed at the age of 89, and in his will, which didn't contain very much, he left a "Stainless Steel 1,000 Poker Chip Set" to "Little Miss René." Her most prized possession.

Soon, Elise started to bring home mysterious amounts of funds from her "part-time job at the mall." But the extra funds helped her parents tremendously, so they held their tongues.

Within a few months, Elise's white bicycle was upgraded to a newer model and gifted to her younger sister. Instead of Yacht Cove, she now ventured into South Carolina's capital city, taking multiple buses to Columbia.

She built up her confidence and her skill, honing card counting techniques and her ability to read her opponent's tells. Whenever she lost, which wasn't very often, she would analyze every aspect of that game and file it away in a mental cabinet of notes.

When Elise was in Grade 10, Grace Point High organized a field trip to Charleston. Many students could not afford the trip fee. Elise jumped at the opportunity. While the teachers led her class around the Battery Promenade and Ravenel Bridge, Elise slipped away to Sullivan's Island – home of South Carolina's celebrity residents.

There, she played for real.

By the time she started Grade 11, Elise had a significant savings account to accompany her stellar academic record. Of course, she had been careful to hide her sinful alter ego from friends and teachers. Her family, she figured, were probably aware.

At 16, Elise asked Louie for career advice. He said, "Darlin,' you're an ace with cards. But gamblin' ain't about how well you play the games. It's about how you handle your money."

That year, she applied to five Ivy League business schools. In the fall, she kissed her folks goodbye, bid farewell to Louie, and boarded a plane to bound to Pennsylvania.

Elise did not particularly like Philadelphia. She found it to be crowded, polluted, and loud. The air was hard to breathe, and temperatures dropped dramatically. Her impression of the Wharton School of Business was not much better. She missed her senior friends and her family, longing for the warmth of South Carolina.

Above all else, Elise especially despised networking. Her face-reading talent became a huge disadvantage in these faux-friendly conversations as she quickly realized that everyone hated everyone else.

She wandered through cocktails and meet & greets, handshakes and business cards, slowly unraveling into a puddle of disillusionment.

Until she met *her*.

- Philadelphia, Pennsylvania. Winter 2006 -

Park Avenue Banquet Hall lit up with dainty golden lights and dazzling evening gowns at the annual Wharton Outstanding Alumni Gala.

After the third keynote speaker, some sleazy politician, she thought, Elise was desperately trying to get the attention of a wine glass-carrying waiter.

Once she succeeded, Merlot in hand, she made a beeline for the wall.

"Hey! Watch it!"

In her hurry, Elise inadvertently cut someone off. The dark red wine she had so eagerly anticipated gulping down was in the process of permanently staining the lace-trimmed ivory gown of a tall, slender woman that stood before her.

The woman's smoky black eyes focused on the growing stain. Elise focused on it too, the emerging crimson pattern along the curve of her hips, and the way her long, dark hair dipped all the way past them.

She quickly threw a hand over her mouth, suddenly unable to process her thoughts.

"Oh, my god – I'm so sorry!" Elise managed. "I'm terribly sorry. I can pay for the dry cleaning. Can I help you wipe that up?" She looked around frantically for napkins.

The mystery woman sighed, inspecting the damage. "I doubt this will come out. But you can try." She turned elegantly on her heel and walked to the ladies' room.

Elise followed.

The paper towel dabbing did not accomplish much except to spread the wine stain some more. Elise could not understand why she felt so nervous every time she pressed the napkins to this woman's dress. Was her perfume that intoxicating? Her intense stare?

"What's your name?" The woman asked when Elise threw out the last of the paper towels.

"Elise René," she answered honestly. "If dry-cleaning won't help, I can get you a new dress. How much was it?"

The other watched Elise with a slight glint in her eye. "$7,000."

Elise's mouth fell open.

The woman left the restroom, beckoning Elise to follow. They went to an empty table off to the side of the ballroom.

"I can get that for you," Elise said once she sat down. "I just need some time."

"Are you a student here?" The woman asked, resting her chin on her palm.

Elise nodded. "Are you? What's your name?"

"Juliette," she said.

"What a lovely name!"

"You think so?" Juliette tilted her head slightly. Elise followed the flow of her silky black hair as it slid off her bare left shoulder. "I think your name is quite pretty. Elise. So graceful."

"Really?" The girl blushed. "Sometimes my folks call me 'Elli.'"

Juliette shook her head. "You shouldn't let them do that. Elise suits you."

An attendant in a suit and lanyard approached their table.

"Ms. Mercer? They'll be ready for you in five."

"Thank you," she said. "I suppose I'll need to do something about this wardrobe malfunction." She opened her purse and took out a large grey shawl, wrapping it around her hips to conceal the stain.

"Mercer," Elise repeated to herself. "Juliette Mercer?" She studied the youthful face of the woman across the table. "As in the youngest US Attorney ever Juliette Mercer?"

Juliette stood.

"Wait," Elise exclaimed, uncertainty in her voice. "What about your dress? I can repay you for it, somehow.

Please." Between her words hung the question, *can I see you again?*

With a brief smile, Juliette slid a glossy slate business card adorned with a number of 7's across the table. The response *call me* drifted in her silence as she turned to leave.

Elise would recall this encounter as the night that changed her life.

She soon began an internship at the United States Attorney's Office in the Eastern District of Pennsylvania, as a direct junior consultant to Attorney Mercer on financial and white-collar crimes.

Her first big break came when her research helped take down two senior city officials for fraud and embezzlement.

Elise was thrown into an overwhelming world. Frozen to the wooden chair against her back, the marble floor beneath her feet, she stared, mesmerized, as Juliette Mercer dissected witnesses one after another. Cold, calculating, ruthless. Beautiful.

Some people drift, others fall. Elise tumbled and collapsed, as one would over the roaring edge of a waterfall, head over heels for the prosecutor.

Elise's small circle of local friends caught wind of her internship and cautioned her against it. Juliette Mercer was famous among her peers and rivals – for her age and talent, of course, but also questionable methods. The heartless prosecutor, Merciless Mercer.

And Elise had heard her fair share of rumors about Juliette even before the winter gala. Rumors of falsified evidence to maintain a perfect guilty record. Rumors of manipulating judges and juries to make her case. Rumors of that sort.

She figured they must be jealous. A young, talented

woman, rising in the ranks to become Attorney General? Surely her competition would try to slander her name! But she was also cast deep under the spell of a little thing called love.

After many months together, Elise told Juliette everything about herself. Her dreams, her past. She shamefully told her about the late nights spent playing poker in squalid bars and proudly about her family back home in White Rock. She even showed her the treasured poker set she got from Max.

Juliette would listen wordlessly, playing with the girl's yellow curls. She never revealed a single detail about her life.

- Philadelphia, Pennsylvania. Summer 2008 -

On a hot August day, two years later, Elise set out on a mission. Their latest case involved a Philadelphia-wide crime ring, run by an organized syndicate that continuously evaded the grasp of the law. They would narrowly slip through the courts because of loopholes or dubious testimony, stirring up a fervor in the city and damaging Mercer's reputation.

Desperate for results, Elise went undercover, hoping to find some solid evidence.

She didn't know if this plan would work, but she had faith, as she did in all of Juliette's ideas.

Elise infiltrated smoothly, and the morning faded into the afternoon without a hitch. This Philly group worked closely with a partner in New Jersey, and she needed to obtain hard proof of their money laundering or other fraud.

That evening, the hideout below the group's Cedar Park

Café was discovered by Philadelphia PD and ample evidence was recovered from the scene.

Elise didn't realize the plan was meant to move so quickly, but she was relieved to have succeeded in her mission. Her relief soon gave way to annoyance as the police arrested her on the spot as well. She tried to explain but was told to 'save it for the judge.'

After an uncomfortable night in custody, Elise was eager to see the familiar face of her mentor and boss in the courtroom. She would clear up the misconceptions in no time at all.

The South Carolina girl took the stand, saying her name:

Elise René
Repeating her plea:
Not guilty

Waiting for the decadent moment she could return to Juliette's side and proclaim victory over these criminal scumbags.

But the moment never came.

Juliette's smoky black eyes, sharp as ever, took aim at the witness stand.

"You were arrested at the scene of the crime, Ms. René. Is that correct?"

"Well, yes, but—"

"Just a yes will suffice, thank you."

Her silky-smooth voice, with its hints of a slight foreign accent, which Elise adored so much, morphed into a menacing creature before her very eyes.

"Your Honor, the café hideout was not the only location in which Ms. René operated."

"What are you talking about? I'm not a part of this gang, I'm just a student!"

"Your Honor, ladies and gentlemen of the jury, I'd like to direct your attention to this piece of evidence we discovered in the syndicate's primary venue."

The twelve heads of the jury turned to the prosecutor's bench as she retrieved a container labeled Exhibit A.

Chest tight, eyes wide, the southern girl's heart shattered at the sight.

"Obtaining this led to the discovery of their underground operation, which allowed us to finally make the arrests we needed to shut them down. It was our foot in the door, so to speak."

Frozen to the wooden chair against her back, the marble floor beneath her feet, Elise stared, terrified, as Juliette Mercer presented a stainless steel 1,000-piece poker set.

Cold, calculating, ruthless. Sinister.

The rumors were true, she realized. And, she soon realized, this case stood between Eastern District of Pennsylvania US Attorney Mercer and Deputy Attorney General of the United States Mercer.

Elise, along with twenty-two members of the Philadelphia crime family, were sentenced to years in jail.

In her state of despair, Elise barely noticed the prison bus taking a detour over the Ben Franklin bridge and into the forests of New Jersey. The bus stopped. Elise found this strange, especially as all the other inmates-to-be were fast asleep. She began to panic when the driver walked up to her seat.

"No need to fret, Miss." He uncuffed her wrists and ankles. "Sorry about the desolate locale, but I got the word last minute."

"What's going on?" She asked cautiously. "What word? Did Juliette clear my name?"

The driver laughed loud enough to wake the other passengers. But they didn't stir.

"Oh, no. You can go, though," he said.

Elise rubbed her wrists. "I don't understand. Why?"

"Best you don't ask too many questions. Best you don't go home, either. Stay out of sight, if you catch my drift. Go on, now," he nudged her to the door.

She stumbled forward but headed to the exit. "You know I'm innocent, right?"

"Look Miss, I just do what I'm told. A big name from Manhattan pulled some strings to get you out, so I guess either they think you are, or they want to stick it to Mercer. Beats me. Now go!"

And so, Elise became a fugitive. She disappeared into the background of New York, later fleeing to Canada then back down to Michigan and Illinois. She resurfaced a year later as Elli.

Sebastian had asked her, a few days after they met, over a shared pot of sweet tea, if she would like to get her revenge on the person that wronged her. She told him the story but excluded locations and details.

"Tell me her name," he said. "We can avenge you."

Elli had looked down, tears threatening to gloss over her eyes. "That's what I'm afraid of," she said. "I think I still love her."

And they left it at that.

TEN

BEHIND THE VEIL

It's evening.

Noa stands in a colorless hallway. The hallway is empty, lined with plain windows that threaten to crack from the rain that shatters upon them.

He begins to walk forward, and each step feels as if it weighs a hundred pounds. The marble floor echoes his footsteps in a way that makes them seem much too loud.

*Step, step, step, step, **step**.*

There is a turn at the end of the hallway. The corners of the walls bend from the light. With the destination in mind, Noa tries to walk faster but it is impossible. A minute feels like an hour and an hour feels like a year.

The rain patters harder; water starts to leak from the cracks in the glass, but doesn't reach the wooden floors. Finally turning the corner, Noa breathes a sigh of relief. There is a golden door visible at the end of the hall and it appears to be close; to be real.

The black steel door is large but not threateningly so. It is a vision of promise and a vision of hope and it's oh so close at the end of the hallway.

The rays of the morning sun hit his face as his walk evolves into a run. His shoes hit the marble faster and faster – his lungs develop a dull ache from rapid breathing.

Run, run, run, run, **run**.

At last, Noa stands in front of the silver door and it suddenly seems much larger and much more intimidating.

Suddenly, he is hit with unspeakable fear. From beyond the door comes a knock. Faint and small, but he can hear it. And it's coming from the door.

The tattered handle of the door beckons him but he doesn't want to open it. He wants to turn around and run back through the hallway, as far away from this door as possible. He looks back, but the hallway is no longer there.

He's facing infinite darkness and it threatens to swallow him whole if given the chance. His heart is beating unsteadily fast. He can't go back.

Instead, Noa reaches for the doorknob.

No, he shouts, **I don't want to open it!**

But he hasn't a choice. His shaking hand grabs hold of the knob and after an eternity it turns in his grip.

He knows what he will see once the door opens but he doesn't want to know. It swings open and his world collapses from the sight that stands before him.

No, he shouts, **I don't want to go in there!**

But he hasn't a choice. One foot steps in front of the other, again and again. Noa freezes as the walls start to shake and his head swarms with voices.

Stop, he calls out, **who's there?!**

He's shaking now, along with the walls, as the door shuts with a bang. A rumble echoes from behind him and he knows what he will feel in a heartbeat.

Crimson flames envelop his body and the smoke chases

after him like a burning shadow. He gasps for air and his eyes widen in terror.

Less than ten steps in front of him, the floor collapses into a blazing inferno. The dark abyss swirls and thrashes against the shaking walls as it rises higher and higher.

Noa is trapped and he can't move. His feet are glued to the only step that hasn't been engulfed in fire and fallen away. His eyes shut as the ground beneath him crumbles.

And he's

f

  a

    l

      l

        i

          n

            g.

He looks down and regrets it immediately.

Awaiting him at the end of the fall are thousands of thousands featureless faces.

Please**, he begs, **please let me go.

He shuts his eyes again and prepares for the impact. He covers his ears, but he can't stop the shouting and screaming and crying that reverberates from the walls around him and resonates through his head.

And all at once, he
lands.

\- Niagara Falls. February 12, 2014 -

Noa jolted up with a gasp. His heart pounded intensely in his chest and his hair clung to the sweat on his face. He was on... a couch?

"Hi there. That's some nightmare; you're pale as a ghost. You alright?"

Noa snapped back to reality, trying to locate the source of the voice. He rubbed his eyes under his glasses and looked around the room.

He was in an office. There was a large wooden desk at the opposite end of the room, and Sebastian was leaning against it, watching him intently with a curious gaze.

"I'm... where?" Noa asked, unable to speak in grammatically correct sentences yet.

Sebastian smiled. "You're in my office. You hit your head."

Noa blinked. Slowly, his memory returned. Elli's phone call, the woman, the gift cards, the elevator, the sixth basement floor. The conversation behind the double doors.

The Niagara Co.

He immediately assumed the worst. Here he was, in the office of, likely, one of the leading members. He was discovered in their hidden lair, eavesdropping on a meeting.

Preparing for the worst, Noa sat up. His hand instantly shot up to his aching head.

This is it, he thought, *this is how I die.*

To Noa's surprise, the voice of the presumed mafia boss was remarkably warm.

"Do you want some water?" Sebastian offered. "Chocolate milk? Juice?"

Noa nodded, immediately regretting it. "Some water. Please."

"Sure." Sebastian poured a glass of water from a pitcher on his desk, handing it to Noa as he pulled up a chair to sit across from the couch.

Noa drank the water cautiously, studying the other man's features. He was young, maybe even younger than thirty. He had intensely fierce blue eyes that unsettled Noa as they held his gaze.

But his face didn't betray any emotions, and Noa couldn't figure out whether the expression was kind, neutral or hostile. They sat in a silence for a few moments. It was Sebastian who broke the stillness by clearing his throat.

"So, Noa." He sat back in the chair. "Let's talk."

Noa gulped, clutching the glass of water a little too tightly. "Okay."

"I'd like for you to tell me how you got down to the sixth floor. Be as thorough as possible in your recollections." Sebastian's voice was calm but coercive.

"Well," Noa started from the beginning, "Elli told me to watch the shop because she had to go to the back. Then this angry lady came in and she wanted to get a gift card. And I'm like, 'we have gift cards?' So, I wanted to find Elli to ask her, but she wasn't in the back room."

Sebastian nodded, "go on."

"I decided to look around myself because the lady was in a hurry. I searched the shelves and there was something that felt like a card, so I pulled on it, but nothing happened. I almost gave up, but then I checked the elevator again, and wouldn't you know it, there were all these floors below ground now! I thought maybe Elli was on a different floor, so I went down."

Sebastian nodded again, "and the sixth floor?"

Noa didn't want to reveal that he used the flash of his phone. It would seem like he was investigating. Which he was. "I just tried random floors till I heard someone talking."

"I see." Sebastian leaned in slightly. "And what, exactly, did you hear of our conversation?"

Noa chose his next words carefully. "Not much, it was

pretty muffled. Something about stalks and *Naz Ducks?*"
He put a finger to his chin, as if trying to remember.

Sebastian laughed, leaning back in the chair again.

Noa heaved a mental sigh of relief.

"Naz Ducks, huh?" Sebastian repeated. "What do you suppose that means?"

Noa shrugged innocently, "I don't know. Is it code for something?"

"Perhaps. Did you hear anything else?"

"Not really. What were you guys discussing?" Noa tried.

"Don't worry about that." Sebastian got up, walking over to his desk.

Noa felt an opportunity. He blurted out, "are you really the Polar Parlor's hiring manager? Why are there so many floors under an ice cream shop?"

The other man turned back. "Oh? You have your doubts, do you?"

"I-I mean no disrespect." Noa fidgeted with the glass. "I just thought things like hidden underground floors only existed in James Bond movies."

"Why don't you tell me what you think, Noa?" Sebastian said. "If not an ice cream shop, then what?"

"Me?" Noa pointed at himself. "Hm. Some kind of secret organization?"

Sebastian smiled. "Close."

Noa stayed seated on the couch, taking in the situation. He wasn't sure how to proceed. Would Sebastian let him go? Erase his memory somehow? Would he kill him?

"Tell me, Noa. Do you have any worthwhile talents?"

As Sebastian said this, the boy started to pick up his tendency to use people's names in conversation. Likely an intimidation tactic. He also noted the leather gloves that never left his hands and what looked like a rosary around his neck, mostly hidden by the shirt collar.

"What do you mean?" Noa asked, trying and failing again to read his expression.

"You are a Polar Parlor employee." Sebastian said. "Which, by extension, makes you my employee. Which, again by extension, makes you a part of the covert operations that run beneath the Parlor's floors."

Noa couldn't believe what he was hearing. "You're saying... What are you saying?"

"Ah, my apologies," Sebastian shook his head lightheartedly. "You don't even know who we are! How rude of me."

Noa held his breath.

Sebastian placed a hand over his chest with a curt bow. "We are the Niagara Company."

———

[AK | 08:10 AM] Hi Agent. Please report on your status.
[NS | 08:11 AM] hello I have located the Niagara co
[NS | 08:11 AM] I think
[NS | 08:12 AM] infiltrated one of their front businesses. Currently undercover
[AK | 08:13 AM] That's fantastic! What is their location?
[NS | 08:13 AM] permission to keep location classified for now
[NS | 08:14 AM] until I am certain
[NS | 08:14 AM] sir
[AK | 08:15 AM] Okay, permission granted. Are you safe?

```
[NS | 08:15 AM] yes. I'm posing as a local
high schooler
[NS | 08:16 AM] finished falsifying docu-
ments this AM in case they look into me
[NS | 08:16 AM] staying at place nearby —
will need to charge for rent
[AK | 08:17 AM] Alright, we'll sort it out.
What is your estimated completion date?
[NS | 08:17 AM] undetermined… possibly
month or so
[AK | 08:18 AM] Great. Continue with
regular updates, Agent.
```

Noa was ecstatic. He shut his laptop cheerfully and removed the ice pack from the bump on his head. A small price to pay, he thought, for the opportunity to infiltrate one of the most notorious crime organizations in history.

He smiled to himself imagining the bonus he was sure to receive upon completing his mission. He also considered thanking the omnipresent deity of Father Emilio's insistent ravings that he forgot his backpack in the hotel room yesterday.

Noa figured they must have searched him, since for some odd reason, his carton of cigarettes was missing. If they found any of his work devices and happened to break into them – he shivered at the thought.

Packing up his few possessions, Noa left the hotel. He moved into a small studio apartment near Hyde Park that day, and, upon settling in, considered his next move.

He didn't have much evidence. Any, really. It would have been great if Noa could have recorded Sebastian's confession, but he couldn't dwell on it now. Instead, he started up files for each of the Niagara Co's alleged members. Elli's file had the most information so far. Sebastian's had the least.

Noa hesitated. There was something about him that didn't sit right with the young agent. A familiar feeling in his stomach he couldn't identify. He shook his head. His primary mission was finding out how they got the stock information.

The chase had begun.

ELEVEN
ST. ISIDORE: PART I. LIGHTHOUSE

- Monaco. Fall, 1994 -

"Okay, my turn. What scares you the most?"

"Drowning." A beat. "And dreaming."

"Dreaming?"

"I drown in my dreams, too." Another pause. "What about you?"

"Hmm." A contemplative stroke of the chin. "Nothing scares me."

An incredulous scoff. "Liar."

Lucciana's lighthouse stood alone on the tip of an abandoned pier. Two young boys, around 8 or 9 years old, sat back-to-back on a wooden crate by the southward window.

One of them, the shorter one, pushed a few stray blond hairs out of his eyes.

"Your turn," he said.

The boys would sneak away in the early hours of dawn to their secret hideout, careful to avoid the headmasters' watchful eyes, and climb the 70 steps to the top.

Leaning against the crumbling brick ledge of the

windowpane, they watched the sunrise over the waves crawling up the Mediterranean coastline.

The taller one, a thin boy with dark hair, thought for a moment. "Who's your least favorite Saint?"

The blond boy shook his head, "I don't believe in that stuff. St. Isidore, I suppose, for obvious reasons. Ask something else."

"Interesting," his friend muttered, "I would have chosen Isidore too."

"Why?"

"The bees. Those evil bugs are one of his symbols, and I'm allergic," he said.

"Huh," the other hummed. "That's why the garden is always swarming with bees? You Catholics are nuts. Ask something else."

"Okay, I've got one. What's your real name?"

A pause. "Are we allowed to say?"

"I won't tell if you won't. Please?" The taller one insisted.

"Fine, but then you say too." The shorter one looked around.

"What is it?"

"Misha." An uncomfortable silence. "Now you."

"Sebastian."

A stillness lingered in the tight quarters of the lighthouse. Neither of them spoke for a few minutes, letting their freshly escaped secrets hang in the air around them.

"What do you miss the most, Sebastian?"

"Just one thing? If I had to choose... Probably my mama's cooking," he said fondly. "Who do you miss the most, Misha?"

"Definitely my little sister. Her name was Katya. She

loved to dance; wanted to be a ballerina." He paused. "She's dead, though."

"Oh. I'm sorry."

Another fleeting moment of tense quiet, broken by the squawk of a passing seagull.

Finally, "Where are you from?" asked Misha. "I mean, where did they find you?"

"Guess," Sebastian replied.

Misha smirked, hopping off the crate. He circled around to face his companion, crossing his arms in an attempt to look serious.

"Easy," he said. "White but tanner than me, dark hair, Latin name. My guess: *Italiano?*"

Sebastian huffed, "There's no way you guessed that just by looking at me!"

"What can I say? I'm a pro." He grinned. "Also, you speak Italian in your sleep."

"Cheater." Sebastian leaned back on the crate. "Okay, let me try. Yellow hair, blue eyes, somewhat short, and you look like a girl. I'd guess German or Swedish, but your name makes me think Eastern European."

Misha frowned. "I do not look like a girl. And I'll get taller!"

"Also," Sebastian added, "you swear in Russian when you think you're alone."

"*Blyat'*, you got me," Misha shrugged. "Where in Italy are you from?"

"That's two questions in a row, but fine. Marghera, Venice. You?"

"Leningrad."

"Isn't it St. Petersburg now?"

"Oh, whatever. Yeah." Misha sat on the crate beside his friend again.

Sebastian leaned his head against the brick of the lighthouse wall. "I'd like to go there, one day."

"I can take you," Misha said eagerly. "I'll show you the Winter Palace and my favorite gardens."

"We can get there through the Baltic sea," Sebastian said. "And then the Neva river. We can see the famous Cruiser Aurora."

Misha raised a brow. "The what? Oh, you mean *Kreysir Avrora.*" He considered this. "I thought you were scared of drowning."

"I am," Sebastian said, "but it's worth the risk to get away. And I bet the stars are so much brighter out at sea."

Misha nodded. "We'll steal a boat, then. When we're big enough. Then we'll—"

He stopped midsentence. The two boys turned to face the stairwell, from which clanged the sound of little shoes climbing rusted steps.

"Well, well," a young girl stuck her head into the room. She had long, silky black hair pulled back into a neat braid. "September and November, running off as usual."

"Piss off, July!" Misha threw a pebble in her direction.

July stuck out her tongue. "You're in trouble for missing mass. But if you want to keep sitting around here, I guess I'll tell the headmaster about your stupid hideout."

"We're coming, shut up already," Sebastian groaned.

The 14th Generation July descended back down the 70 steps, reluctantly followed by the 14th Generation November and September.

Under his breath, September whispered to November, "we need a new hideout."

- Niagara Falls. February 13, 2014 -

A knock sounded on a metal office door, 14 floors below the Polar Parlor. Then, a voice through the intercom.

"Boss? Lucy and I went to the Starbucks, y'know, the one she was banned from? The new manager was so scared; he gave us like a year's supply. Want some?"

Sebastian unlocked the door with a button on the desk's underside without looking up from his computer. "Come in."

The door hissed open and Mike stepped inside with a tray of coffee cups, placing one on the large desk. "It's mocha – that's the one you like, right?"

"Thanks," Sebastian said, taking the cup. "Anything to report?"

Mike sat in a chair across from him, taking a coffee for himself. "I think Elli finished up the year-end report yesterday. She said something about 'cross border synergy' and other made-up words. She may have mentioned horses?"

"Mm." Sebastian still didn't look up. "What about Noa?"

"He's doing well!" Mike said. "He really is good with computers, like he said. I think he set up some kind of new security system for the staff access door last week. Not sure how it works yet though, and I got locked out a couple times. Other than that, I think—"

He was cut off by the sound of the door, which Mike had forgotten to close upon coming in, swinging open.

"Boss," Nick hurried inside, closing the door behind him. "We got trouble."

Sebastian temporarily glanced away from the screen. "Where?"

"Washington. But we're also picking up some weird info about your old fightin' grounds," he said.

"Manhattan?" Mike asked, surprised.

Nick nodded.

Sebastian spun the chair away from the computer. "Interesting. I'll deal with Manhattan later. Can you tap your Sacramento contact for now? I'm assuming Washington is having trouble accepting the terms of our agreement."

"I'll see what I can do," Nick said, cracking his fingers. "What's the negotiatin' limit?"

Sebastian considered it for a moment. "Within the bounds of the bridal veil reserves. But try to keep it reasonable, would you?"

Nick grinned, "Don't I always?" Before he turned to leave, his hand hesitated over the door handle. "One more thing, Boss."

"What is it?" Sebastian returned to his computer, idly tapping on the rim of the coffee cup while his eyes scanned the screen.

"I don't really trust that kid," he said. "It's just—well. He came out of nowhere, is all I'm saying. Is it safe to have him around?"

Mike flung his arm around Nick's shoulder. "Aw, lighten up! He's just a kid. Plus he's a complete tech nerd. Did you see the new security system he made? And he's building some kind of ice cream robot for Elli."

"Whatever," Nick removed Mike's arm. "I'm just saying."

Sebastian listened passively. "Keep an eye on Noa, if you'd like. Show him the veil and see how he reacts."

Nick grinned. "You got it, Boss."

"What're you working on?" Mike peered over the monitor after Nick had left.

"National expansion," Sebastian said. "We need to throw the feds off our trail now that the border consolidation is within our grasp."

"Sounds like a good plan to me!" Mike said with a nod. "You always know what to do."

"Ready?" Elli asked with excited anticipation. "Three... two..."

"One!" Noa flipped the switch on a small makeshift remote, and the Polar Parlor's interior rumbled with a mechanical force.

Behind the counter, the first prototype of PecanBot whirred to life with an electrical hum as its metal limbs sprang into action towards the tub of chocolate ice cream.

"Oh, dear," Elli exclaimed. "Too fast, too fast!"

The machine scooped the dessert with such force that it flew straight up, sticking to the ceiling. Excess chocolate ice cream dripped down to the counter and the floor.

"Crap." Noa powered down the prototype. "I'll fix that," he added sheepishly.

Elli laughed, just as Nick entered the Parlor through the employee door. "Maybe we can use Pecan as a weapon?" she said. "Nicky can be our practice dummy!"

"If you two are done goofing off," he said, "I need the kid."

Elli's smile disappeared. "Why? Where are you taking him?"

Noa felt a tension materialize between them.

He had been an unofficial-official member of the

Niagara Co. for just under a week, but still spent most of his time with Elli. Sometimes with Mike, though he still couldn't figure out his role considering his air of aloofness.

Nick tended to avoid him, except for the occasional suspicious glare. Lucy, which he gathered to be the name of a fifth mysterious local member, he had yet to even meet. But from his brief interactions with Mike, Noa gathered that the guy fancied Lucy quite a bit.

"Does it matter where I'm takin' him?" Nick said, passing Elli and gripping Noa by the arm. "I'm just going to show him the ropes is all. You want to see the ropes, don't you, kid?"

Noa tried to flinch out of his grasp but was unable. "Now? I guess, but I—"

Elli slammed her apron down on the counter. "Let him go, Nick. Does Bassie know about this?"

"He sure does," Nick released Noa's arm but pushed him towards the back door with the motion. "We'll be at the veil if you need us."

"Fine," Elli crossed her arms. A worried expression passed over her face. "I'll be waiting. This bot won't fix itself, sugar."

Noa felt instinctively uneasy as Nick went through the staff-only door and motioned for him to do the same. He half-smiled at Elli and waved goodbye, following Nick out of the Parlor.

They entered the elevator in a tense silence. Nick activated the button for the -5 floor.

Noa fiddled with the ends of his sweater sleeves nervously. What did Nick mean by 'the veil?'

The elevator opened to a long, winding hallway.

"Out you go, kid." Nick said.

Noa stepped out obediently. He desperately needed

some kind of evidence to report back to his superiors, but he had to be careful around Nick. He was the oldest of the members that Noa met so far, and definitely the most suspicious.

At a minimum, Noa wanted to figure out this local team's identities. It was clear they wouldn't be sharing their insider trading business with him anytime soon – he'd need to worm his way into that once he gained their trust.

"Where are we going?" Noa asked casually. "Is it outside? I didn't bring my coat," he said, peering down the long hallway. It seemed to extend for an unusually long distance, before curving southwards.

"We're not goin' outside." Nick stopped in front of a door that resembled a utility closet and unlocked it, retrieving two large, empty suitcases. He rolled one to Noa. "Get moving."

Noa took up the suitcase, pulling it behind as he kept walking down the hall with Nick at his heels. He glanced back at the luggage, recognizing it after a brief moment. They were the same suitcases that Mike dragged in, stuffed to the brim, the night Noa first met him and Sebastian. Noa tried to recall that interaction, but all he could remember was Mike's boisterous greeting and prompt exit with the bags.

The hallway curved, and Noa's step wavered as a kilometer of fluorescent-lit tile opened up before him. Nick stumbled onto the suitcase behind Noa.

"The hell? What's the hold up? I didn't tell ya to stop."

"How long does it go?" Noa marveled.

"Doesn't concern you," Nick said. "Now move it."

They continued down the hall for about fifteen minutes. Gradually, Noa felt a soft vibration developing as he walked. He glanced up at the ceiling. The lights flickered ever so slightly. As they continued, a constant hum could be heard through the walls. It sounded like a muffled thunder, looping endlessly on the lowest volume. The vibrations intensified.

Noa visualized a city map in his mind. His grip tightened on the luggage handle when his logic reluctantly confirmed that which his gut had been screaming for the past few minutes.

They were under the falls.

The tracker he planted on Elli wasn't faulty after all, he realized, when her pink GPS dot migrated over the waters despite the fact that she never went outside or got in a car. She must have taken this hallway.

But then, he recalled, *it must connect to the Bella Luna too!* Elli's movements went first to the winery and then to the falls. *How large is this underground maze?*

The hall at last opened to a rounded chamber. There were a series of doors, each with a different label. Noa committed them to memory.

Luna. Bird. Green. Robinson. Goat. Three Sisters. Brother. Bridal Veil. Canada. America.

He knew these names. They appeared on his map as well – they were the islands and waterfalls on the Niagara River.

"This way," Nick said, passing him on the way to the door marked 'Bridal Veil.'

The veil. Noa hurried after him. "What is this place?"

Nick paused at the door, turning to face him. "You ask a lotta questions, kid. How about I ask a question. Do you know what happens when someone takes a tumble into the falls?"

Noa swallowed uncomfortably. "I imagine it's not very pleasant? Sir."

Nick leaned down slightly to meet Noa's eye-level. "The first thing you'd feel is the terror. Facing the edge of a 60-foot drop, freezin' cold rapids of the Hell's half acre pushing you 70 miles an hour. Next is suffocation. When you hit the bottom, assuming you didn't fall headfirst and break your neck, the metric tons of water pressure from above and swirling around will drown you."

Noa shivered. That did sound unpleasant.

"If, by some miracle," Nick continued, "you survived the fall itself, this is when the hypothermia kicks in. You'll be banged up and disoriented. And slowly freeze to death, swept away to a watery grave."

Unsure if he should respond, Noa just stood on the spot.

"We call this place our own lil' Hell's half acre," Nick added, with something sinister creeping into his voice. "Wanna know why?"

"Um," Noa's voice cracked. "Why?"

"Few reasons," he said. "There's a passage out from here straight to those rapids, just upstream the falls. When we think someone might be a threat to the organization," he reached into the inner pocket of his white suit, "I escort them there."

Noa paled when he suddenly met eyes with the barrel of a gun.

"So, kid," Nick said calmly. "Before you ask any more questions, I've got one more for you. Are you a threat to the organization?"

The boy shook his head vigorously, kicking himself mentally for losing yet another avenue. "No, sir!"

"Great," Nick put the gun away, straightening his jacket. "But I've got my eye on you. The Boss might have a soft spot for dreamers or Catholic repentance or whatever, but not me."

Leaving Noa temporarily frozen in place from his near-death encounter, Nick unlocked a series of locks on the door marked 'Bridal Veil' and stepped inside.

"Well? You comin' or what?"

Breaking out of his stupor, Noa followed. Behind what he could only assume was the Bridal Veil waterfall stood a massive vault, well over 300 feet tall.

"Whoa," Noa could not prevent his shock from escaping. "That is massive!"

Obscuring the lock from view, Nick entered a lengthy combination. He spun the wheel of the vault and it slowly popped open with a hiss.

This time, Noa's jaw simply dropped open.

While Nick made quick work loading up the suitcases, Noa gawked at the contents of the vault in bewilderment.

"Mr. Nick," he said timidly. "May I ask just one question?"

"What?" Nick grunted.

"Is this," Noa gestured to the mountains of cash in varying currencies, "all of Niagara Co.'s money?"

Nick simply laughed in response, zipping up the first suitcase and getting started on the second.

Unbelievable, Noa thought. *How in the world did they get so rich?*

TWELVE

ST. ISIDORE: PART II. ROSARY

- Monaco. Summer, 1998 -

"I said, close them!" Misha chastised jokingly, hiding his hands behind his back.

"Am I going to regret this?" Sebastian asked, reluctantly closing his eyes. "If you push me in, I'll die."

The two boys sat on the wooden boardwalk of the Jardin Japonais, hours after it had closed to the public, feet dangling over the ledge of the murky green pond.

"Okay, open." Misha held his hand out, revealing a small box in his palms.

"What is this?" Sebastian peaked with one eye.

"Happy birthday, Sebby!" The blond exclaimed.

The other boy took the box hesitantly. "How do you know it's my birthday?"

"I snuck into Emilio's office," Misha said. "And there we all were. Our miserable lives wrapped up in manila folders."

"You're insane – what if he caught you?" Sebastian started unwrapping the gift. "Or would he let you off easy because of your high potential?"

"Ugh." Misha made a disgusted face. "The word 'potential' must've been written 10 times in my file."

Sebastian lifted the lid of the box. "Oh, wow. This is... wow."

The other boy smiled. "You like it? I figured, since you actually believe in this stuff."

Sebastian gently lifted a delicate, baroque-style rosary. "I love it. Thank you."

They shared a comfortable silence, watching the Koi fish float past in the lantern light.

"When's your birthday?" he asked, running his fingers along the beads of the rosary.

"It's in the spring," Misha said. "But you don't have to get me anything."

"That's up to me," Sebastian replied, with a slight smile. "What do you think you'll be doing ten years from now?"

"Hmm," Misha pondered aloud, kicking his legs over the water. "The old fart wants to fast-track me up some corporate conglomerate hellhole so I can keep sponsoring this place. I'm more interested in law. Maybe."

"I think the oligarch lifestyle would suit you," Sebastian said.

"Piss off. What about you?"

Sebastian looked down at the necklace in his palms. "I don't know. I want to see the world; maybe make a difference in my own, small way."

Misha pouted. "I like your answer better. Can I come with you?"

The taller boy laughed, "If you want. When? Should we run? To St. Petersburg, like we planned?"

"No," the blond shook his head. "If they suspected anything, I wouldn't want to face the Ingrid's wrath." He shivered, "I'm still recovering from her last 'therapy session'."

"When we graduate, then," Sebastian offered. "We'll need to graduate at the same time, though."

Misha stuck out his hand, "How do you say 'deal' in Italian? I only know the basics."

"*Affare fatto,*" Sebastian shook his hand. "How do you say it in Russian?"

"Affa-ray fat-oh," Misha repeated. "And *dogovorilis'!*"

"..." The Italian boy paused. "It's a deal."

THIRTEEN

CONNECTIONS

- Toronto. February 17, 2014 -

"It's serious then, is it?" Lavoie peered at the screen over her glasses. "That little troublemaker really thinks he's infiltrated the Niagara Co.? How does he even know it's them?"

Koven powered up the secure chat interface on his computer. "He claims he got a personal introduction from a member. And overheard relevant conversations that match our intelligence."

"Fascinating," Lavoie said, unconvinced.

A ping rang out from the laptop.

```
[NS | 09:30 AM] hello sir
[AK | 09:30 AM] Good morning, Noa.
[AK | 09:31 AM] What have you got to
report?
[AK | 09:31 AM] You've been there 2 weeks,
right?
[AK | 09:32 AM] Are you safe?
```

[NS | 09:32 AM] yes… unfortunately not much right now sir

"Shocker," Lavoie remarked, under her breath.
"Just give him a chance, Miriam."

[NS | 09:33 AM] I started files on 5 Niagara Co members
[NS | 09:33 AM] operating from this location
[NS | 09:34 AM] to be frank, they are a bit strange
[AK | 09:34 AM] Strange? What do you mean.
[NS | 09:36 AM] not what I expected
[NS | 09:37 AM] not all of them, at least
[NS | 09:38 AM] there is one woman with financial background
[NS | 09:38 AM] southern, goes by elli
[NS | 09:39 AM] she is the group's accountant of sorts but also runs an ice cream shop
[AK | 09:40 AM] Is she involved in the insider trading?
[NS | 09:41 AM] not sure but would not be surprised
[NS | 09:42 AM] the second woman seems dangerous
[NS | 09:42 AM] think her name is lucy
[AK | 09:43 AM] Any others?
[NS | 09:44 AM] there is also this gangster type guy, from LA or san francisco
[NS | 09:44 AM] don't think he likes me

[NS | 09:45 AM] but the boss's right-hand
man is nice
[NS | 09:45 AM] just seems useless… he
doesn't do anything
[AK | 09:46 AM] He's the right-hand man?
[NS | 09:46 AM] yeah and I have no idea why
[NS | 09:48 AM] from what I gathered, he
lost his whole family and then ended up
working for the boss
[AK | 09:49 AM] Odd.
[NS | 09:50 AM] yeah, like his dad died
from ALS and his sister was shot by a
robber and he almost killed himself but
then he met the boss
[NS | 09:51 AM] now he's just insanely
loyal even though he's useless

"How does any of this help us, Alex?" Lavoie asked semi-rhetorically. "We need to know about the trading."

"I'm curious about this boss he keeps mentioning," Koven said when he finished scribbling down on the notepad.

[AK | 09:53 AM] Interesting. What about the
boss himself?
[NS | 09:54 AM] unfortunately he's a
mystery
[NS | 09:54 AM] he's pretty young consid-
ering the power he seems to wield
[NS | 09:55 AM] his name is Sebastian Nové

but my research didn't reveal much so far
except online rumors
[NS | 09:56 AM] he stays at a distance from
me and the other members… I think there is
a lot that he controls on his own behind
the scenes

Agent Lavoie leaned over the computer, hijacking the
keyboard.

[AK | 09:57 AM] Sounds like he should be
your primary target for investigation
regarding the insider trading, then.
[AK | 09:58 AM] Not the rag-tag group of
pals.
[NS | 10:00 AM] I know sir
[NS | 10:00 AM] but as I said he keeps
everyone at arm's length
[NS | 10:01 AM] I will try

FOURTEEN

ST. ISIDORE: PART III. NIGHT

- Monaco. Winter, 2000 -

Pale snowflakes blanket the ground, shrouding the buildings, palm trees, and cars with an ashen white coat. A rare Siberian cold front drifted into the French Riviera that morning, wrapping the Azure Coast in a frigid, violent embrace.

Inside the town square, a large and imposing Christmas tree shines brilliantly, although Christmas had long since passed.

Flurries of snow dance through the empty streets, picking up gusto in the narrow passageways. It is past midnight, and the town is stationary. A gramophone can be heard somewhere in the distance. The smell of cold and darkness hangs in the air, harsh and imposing.

Footprints in the snow are fading, drowned by fresh layers. Tall streetlamps illuminate the cobblestone street, dim as candlelight.

A boy walks down the path, alone, surrounded by

emptiness. The lamp helplessly shines down the long and winding road. Only the night remains.

He is hard to miss and yet impossible to notice, walking as a shadow towards no destination in particular. By an old streetlight, now unused and broken, his remaining spirit shatters at his feet.

His thoughts spiral mercilessly over and over and over, like a silent scream.

How? How could this happen?

Three words looped endlessly in his mind.

The wrinkled face of the old headmaster as he spoke them.

The wretched silence in that room.

An unbearable, darkening pain washes over him. A cry echoes through the stillness of the night as stray blond locks fall over grieving blue eyes.

Three inescapable, haunting words.

"November is dead."

- Niagara Falls. February 18, 2014 -

Two in the morning. Nothing but the light of the monitor reflecting off his glasses and the harsh glare of the bedside alarm clock. Curtains drawn; surrounded by snacks and a third mug of coffee, now nearly empty.

Noa's comfort zone.

Leaning on a makeshift fortress of discounted pillows against the wall, warmth of the laptop against his legs, the young CSIS agent focused on his research, determined to dig up more information to his employers lest they demand his return.

He already found all that there was to find about the Niagara Co. through conventional means, and none of the members disclosed their full names anyway. Except one.

It was likely fake, but a name was a name, and it may uncover a trail. However, Noa would have to search in the abyss of the deep, dark corners of the web, as the regular research revealed nothing.

He opened an onion router and began his dive.

Sebastian Nové.

Every mention of the name was ghostlike. No tangible trace; no photos; no links to any crimes. Noa managed to pin some geographical attributes in his search, but considering they matched what his team already knew - that is, all around the Great Lakes - it wasn't very valuable knowledge. The only variation was a high concentration of tags in Manhattan around 2007.

The first mention of Sebastian Nové's name, however, broke the monotony.

As early as 2004, there was a reference to an up-and-comer *Nové* in Venice. Never anything concrete, but vague descriptions of a new face appearing at the side of some Venetian crime boss in Italian black-market chat rooms. Circumstantial, at best. Then, a handful of times, the name came up in Murano drug-trafficking sites over the next couple of years.

Noa's head shot up so fast that his vision blurred. Something about that place triggered his memory. He shut his eyes, scouring his mental images for any trace of the word.

Murano... Where would I have seen someone talk about Murano?

Transplanted back to the Starbucks near the Polar Parlor, his eyelids few open.

In a flurry of keystrokes, Noa searched for the tags that

he remembered from the news bulletin of the coffee shop's corner TV.

Murano / body / discovered / February / 2014

2-week-old articles from Italian and other European news sources populated the screen.

As his eyes scanned the text, the events of Friday two weeks back returned to him.

He remembered the boisterous greeting that Mike exclaimed, when he and Sebastian came into the Parlor the night Noa met them for the first time.

Buongiorno.

When the sun shone brilliantly through his window, Noa was awoken by the ringing of the doorbell.

He startled himself upright, realizing that he fell asleep on his glasses, computer in his lap, and that it was already past 9:00 AM. The doorbell rang again.

Who could that be? He only shared his address with Elli, when he still thought she'd be sending him Polar Parlor employee wages.

Acting on instinct, Noa shoved his CSIS laptop under his mattress and hid anything else related to his work out of sight.

"Coming," he called out, attempting to arrange his hair in a way that didn't look like obvious bed head. Straightening out his clothes before the door, he turned the lock and opened it.

"Morning," his visitor said. "Late night?"

Noa felt a bit ill.

"Mr. Nové," he said in a hoarse voice, "good morning. What brings you here?"

"Please, you can call me Sebastian. Can I come in?"

Noa's heart was racing. Was there anything in his apartment that might reveal his identity? Could the crime boss see that he just discovered their murderous cover-up in Venice on his face?

"Yeah—of course," Noa stepped aside a bit too quickly, letting Sebastian through. "Sorry about the mess. I fell asleep watching an X-Files marathon."

"Ah. Well, pardon the intrusion," Sebastian said casually. "Elli informed me of your address. Thought I would stop by."

As always, Noa could not read the intent in those sharp blue eyes. He felt a sense of dread but forced himself to remain calm.

"Right, sure," the young agent said, clearing his throat. "Can I get you anything? Coffee?"

"No, that's fine." Sebastian seemed distracted by his surroundings. Noa nervously followed his line of sight. "You really ought to tidy this place up, Noa," he added unexpectedly.

The boy's face turned red. "Pardon?"

Sebastian gestured around them. "What a mess. You have clothes littered around the floor, dishes everywhere. How old are you? Didn't your parents raise you to clean up after yourself?"

"Sorry," Noa stumbled on his words, reflexively stuffing a few items of clothing into a drawer. "I didn't, um. I guess you could say my parents didn't spend much time with me, growing up."

"Is that so?" Sebastian turned to face him again. "Well. In any case, I wanted to discuss something with you. If you haven't got any plans, we could go for breakfast."

An opportunity to gain some evidence or a possibility of death. Noa nodded eagerly.

"No plans!" He stepped toward the exit and promptly stopped upon catching a glimpse of his reflection in the mirror. "Mind if I just change and freshen up real quick?"

Sebastian leaned against the doorframe, "No rush." He kept his coat and gloves on, waiting patiently until Noa was ready. "Bring your computer," he added just as they were leaving.

Noa grabbed his personal laptop – consciously avoiding eye contact with the mattress – and shoved it in his bag, following Sebastian.

Outside of the apartment building, Noa could only assume the jet-black S-Class Mercedes idling on the curb was waiting for them. His assumption proved correct when

Mike hopped out of the driver's seat and held the passenger door open for Sebastian.

"Hey guys," he said. "Going to Maria's, Boss?"

"Please," Sebastian confirmed.

Noa got in the backseat of the car, curiosity building. This would be his first outing with Sebastian, and he sincerely hoped it would go better than his journey behind the falls with Nick.

Mike made his way from the Hyde Park district down Pine Avenue to Main Street, turning towards the Rainbow International Bridge. Noa peered out the tinted window.

"We're crossing the border?" he asked.

Mike smiled at him through the rearview mirror. "Best breakfast place around Niagara's on the Canadian side."

Noa watched the car in front of them pass through the security checkpoint. "I didn't bring my passport," he said worriedly.

"Don't worry about it," Mike said jovially.

They pulled up to the border patrol gate. Mike rolled his window down.

"Morning, pal," he said to the officer. "Just a quick round trip. Niagara Co. delivery."

"Right," the officer yawned, raising the bar. "Enjoy your trip."

As they drove over the Niagara River, Noa glanced back at the American shore. "Cool," he muttered, unknowingly out loud.

On the Canadian side, Mike stopped the car in front of a chic café in a touristy neighborhood. The sign above read *Queen of Spades*. He got out and opened the door for Sebastian.

"Give me a shout when you're done," he said.

"Shouldn't be long," Sebastian entered the café. "Let's go, Noa."

Noa hurried inside. The cozy restaurant seemed more like a European tearoom, with a red and gold décor and chandelier lighting. It was mostly empty save for a few couples scattered about the tables.

A woman in a waitress uniform approached them with enthusiasm. "Mr. Nové," she exclaimed. "How wonderful to see you." She had an Eastern European accent.

"You as well, Maria," Sebastian said politely.

"Which menu you want today?" she asked, briefly glancing at Noa. "Queen of Spades special or $37 Ace?"

Sebastian removed his coat with a quiet, amused laugh. "The Ace. Thank you."

"What a relief!" Maria said, taking his coat. "Cleaning service not in 'til afternoon. Okay, follow me." She went towards the back of the café.

Noa couldn't help but think he missed some crucial information. He looked to Sebastian, who simply beckoned him to follow Maria.

They went into a separate dining room, lined with bookshelves. Maria stopped before one and pushed on a book, triggering the entire bookcase to turn 180 degrees and open into a private lounge.

"After you," Sebastian said.

"Whoa," Noa went inside, removing his own coat and taking a seat at the hidden table, placing his computer bag beside him. The chairs were soft – paneled with embroidered cushions – and the room itself had a wide array of books and a TV monitor.

"I bring breakfast," Maria said, taking her leave.

"What was that about the specials?" Noa asked once Sebastian sat down as well.

"Two fixed ideas cannot exist in the brain at the same time any more than two bodies can occupy the same point in space," came the vague response.

Noa felt as though he were being tested. "Is that a quote from a book? Or an old play?"

"Very good," Sebastian smiled. "Technically, both. Originally by Russian author Aleksandar Pushkin."

"Pushkin," Noa repeated. "Queen of Spades, right? I think I heard of it."

"Our protagonist, Herman, seduces a young lady with the goal of meeting her elderly guardian – the Countess – for she knows the notorious secret of the *three winning cards* that can win any game." Sebastian said. "However, when she refuses to tell Herman, he accidentally kills her.

"After her funeral, the ghost of the Countess speaks to him: Herman must bet on the three, the seven and the ace," Maria approached with tea and their meal as he continued. "He goes to gamble. On the first night, he bets everything on the three, and wins. On the second night, he bets everything on the seven, and wins.

"On the third night, Herman bets on the ace but realizes he mistakenly bet on the queen of spades instead. The queen, bearing a striking resemblance to the Countess, winks at him," Sebastian concluded with a polite nod to Maria. "Herman loses everything. And spends the rest of his life institutionalized."

Noa nodded, stuffing his mouth unceremoniously with bread. "Sounds about right for a Russian story. So, if we're having the three-seven-ace option, then what's the queen of spades special?"

Maria left, shutting the bookcase behind her.

"What do you think, Noa?" Sebastian asked, pouring himself some tea.

Noa considered the story, and Maria's relief from earlier. He came to an unfortunate conclusion, swallowing the bread with a cough. Coupled with his findings from the early hours of the morning, he felt increasingly trapped in the warm confines of this hidden lounge.

Sebastian watched him with an amused expression. "Are you always this pale, or was it just the X-Files marathon? I imagine you'd have a greater number of freckles with some color in your face."

Noa looked away uncomfortably, wanting nothing more than the cold outdoors and a cigarette. "I tend to stay up late on the computer most nights."

"Ah, that's actually what I was hoping to discuss," Sebastian said. "Mike and Elli tell me you're good with technology. I had a look at the security system you installed at the Parlor."

The boy perked up. "What did you think?"

"Impressive," he replied genuinely. "What gave you the idea?"

Noa poked at an egg, thinking back to his accidental discovery of their underground offices. "I thought it might be a good idea to install a locking mechanism on the back-door and a video feed of the elevator entryway, so that you could always see who's coming and going."

He neglected to add that as the software's creator, he could access and alter it at-will. In case he ever needed to investigate later.

"The lock is a great idea," Sebastian said. "As for the video monitoring, can you view it now? Remotely?"

"Sure," Noa took his computer out, moving some dishes out of the way. "You can too, if you install it on a laptop." He powered up the machine and the software, turning the screen so both of them could see a live feed of the Polar Parlor's back hall.

"Good." Sebastian reached behind him and retrieved a thin PC notebook from beneath some coffee table books. He placed it on the table, facing Noa.

The agent regarded it with some unease. "What's this?"

"Untraceable computer, with access to anything you might need," said Sebastian.

"Anything I might need... for what?"

"To hack the security system you installed."

FIFTEEN

ST. ISIDORE: PART IV. VOID

- Monaco. Spring, 2001 -

The first rays of the sun broke through the stained glass of the old window. Underneath grey blankets, a shifting lump stirred to another dawning of realization.

This cursed orphanage. This tiny room. This miserable life.

After some time, with a yawn, the boy got up from his bed and lazily pulled on his school uniform. The ironed crest of St. Isidore was neatly threaded above his heart. He winced as a screeching noise sounded from a speaker in the corner of his room.

"*Bonjour, buongiorno,* good morning. I trust that you had a restful sleep. Breakfast will be served in 10 minutes; anyone who is late will not eat. *Perfer et obdura, dolor hic tibi proderit olim.*"

Misha had heard this message every single morning for almost a decade.

"September! Are you awake yet?" A knock came from his bedroom door, "Are you coming to breakfast?"

"Soon," he grumbled back at January's eager voice, "I'll be down soon, just piss off." As he heard the footsteps retreating, he continued his morning routine.

He brushed his teeth and ran a comb through tangled yellow hair. It was getting long, but he didn't care enough to cut it. He blew the bangs out of his eyes and retrieved a small jewelry box from a drawer. He pulled out an ornate rosary and hung it around his neck.

Then, as per his recent ritual, he removed the necklace and gently returned it to the drawer, next to a wooden urn. Eventually, he left his room and went down the stairs to the dining hall.

He bumped into the bony shoulder of a tall middle-aged woman, who turned to glare at him.

"And where do you think you're going, *boy*?"

He composed himself, taking a step back. "To eat, Sister Ingrid. Move. *Please*."

"I don't think so." The woman made a dramatic gesture of looking at her watch. "I distinctly remember hearing that breakfast was to be served in ten minutes. That was eleven minutes ago."

"So, what?" Refusing to back down, the boy crossed his arms. "You're not going to let me eat because I'm one minute late?"

Sister Ingrid pushed up her glasses. "Punctuality is very important. Lack of punctuality can lead to chaos. The students of St. Isidore must strive for perfection in all facets of life."

"I think you're confused," Misha said. "Saint Isidore liked *punctuation* not punctuality. That's why he invented the comma."

Sister Ingrid's eye twitched. "Watch your tone, September."

"Whatever. Can I just eat now?"

"Absolutely not," she replied bitterly. "Consider hunger as your punishment. Now I suggest you go to class early and think about what you've done. Be on time for lunch."

Refusing to acknowledge the headmistress's words, the blond turned on his heels and stormed outside to the front yard of the orphanage. He kicked a rock angrily, stuffing his hands into his pockets.

"Having a bad day, September?"

He turned around to see a teenage girl sitting up against a tree, piecing together a colorless puzzle. Her long black hair was tied up in a bun and she was watching him condescendingly with coal-colored eyes.

"Not bad enough to want to talk to you, July," came the harsh reply.

"Oh, come now." She tilted her head to the side, "Who've you got to talk to, now that poor November kicked the bucket?"

Misha's expression darkened. "That's low. Even for you."

"I have no respect for the weak," she said flippantly. "Besides, we both know that *I* will be the first to graduate from Gen. 14. Frankly, I don't know why you're still trying."

"And what then, huh?" Misha's hands curled into fists as he slowly approached July. "You'll go back to North Korea as a professional snitch?"

July didn't look up from her puzzle. "I'm from Busan, you commie asshole. And for the record, I'm going into law, after graduating early."

"Is that so?" Misha bent down to get in her face. "If you're such a stellar student, why are you out here and not inside having breakfast with the others?"

"Isn't it obvious? I already had breakfast with Father Emilio," July said calmly.

"Liar!" In a single swift motion, Misha swiped the milk puzzle with his hand, sending the pieces flying in every direction.

July blinked. "It's your problem if you don't believe me. Either way, you might as well abandon your hopes of surpassing me."

Misha tuned her out, looking up at the sky as July continued to talk.

"—and Father Emilio always says we should be calm and think rationally, even in stressful situations. That's why my ability to contain my emotions makes me so much better than you, September. You get riled up over the smallest things; how can you possibly succeed? Are you even listening to me?" July scowled. "What in the world are you smiling about? Starving to death?"

"Today," Misha paused, "is my birthday."

July was taken aback by this comment. "What? Who the hell cares?" She got up abruptly and left, leaving her puzzle behind.

Misha was alone once again. He sat under the shade of the tree.

"I'm 15 today," he said no one in particular.

He sat outside for hours, missing two classes. He didn't care much about his work, or his 'high potential,' as the headmaster repeatedly told him. The news of November's death brought an end to any hope he had of a bright future, sailing the world.

His thoughts were interrupted by the voices of other children, leaving the classrooms for lunch time break.

"Did you hear?" Two girls walked by him, conversing

loudly with each other. "They're bringing in a new month today."

"Really? That was fast," said the second girl to the first. Misha knew them but not well. May and October.

"I guess, but you know what that means, right?" The first one asked her friend.

"Yeah. The rumors are true. Better watch out for those bees..." The other girl said menacingly, running into the garden.

"Hey, wait!" Her friend followed close behind as they ran off.

Misha stared down at the grass with a hollow expression.

As the afternoon faded, he finally stood and went inside. Eyes fixated on the wooden floors, Misha walked headfirst into Sister Ingrid once again.

"Would you watch where you're going?" Sister Ingrid pushed him back.

"Maybe you shouldn't be standing in the middle of the goddamn hallway," he muttered under his breath, wanting nothing more than to get back to his room.

Ingrid raised her hand, readying a swing. "You little bra—"

"Sister." An older man stopped her wrist midair. "No need for that, I'm sure."

Misha pushed his way past them both without a word.

"You really go too easy on that boy, Father," Ingrid sighed in exasperation. "Is the new child here?"

Father Emilio nodded curtly. "Indeed. The car is pulling up as we speak."

Misha quickly ran upstairs to his room. He felt an inexplicable urge to see the newcomer's arrival for himself. To assess this impostor, coming to steal the name of his dearest friend.

He climbed out his window, onto the lattice of the roof, watching as a black car made its way to the front of the Home. He could barely remember his own arrival. Was it in a car like this one?

It was many years ago, and Misha tried to refrain from remembering his life before St. Isidore. The lesser of two miseries.

He watched as the car's back door opened and a nun stepped out. In one hand, she held a tattered brown messenger bag, charred from flames, probably containing all of the new arrival's belongings.

In the other, she firmly held the tiny hand of a young boy that followed her outside.

Misha squinted, trying to get a better view. He looked to be about five or six years old. A redhead, in an oversized shirt and torn pants with burnt edges, and no shoes.

"Welcome to St. Isidore," he heard the Sister say. "November."

A reluctant sigh and a long pause preceded a triple knock on the headmaster's ornate oak door at the end of the hall.

"Come in, September."

With a creaky disobedience, the door eased open slowly. The boy known as 14th Generation September stepped inside.

Father Emilio was seated behind a large wooden desk, his face betraying no sign of emotion. Before him, in one of the cushion-backed chairs, quietly sat a small, red-haired boy.

He was staring out the window. No, September thought, it looked as though the child was fixated upon the window itself. His big, dark green eyes looked vacant.

They had changed him out of the burnt clothes he wore when he arrived. A crisp, freshly pressed St. Isidore uniform hugged his tiny frame. The grey fabric made the fiery color of his hair more vibrant – September had never seen a color like that before.

"September, meet our newest student," Father Emilio said. "This is November the 15th."

"Right," the blond responded bitterly. "And what does that have to do with me?"

"As you know, we are all very heartbroken by the passing of the elder November," Emilio crossed himself with a whispered prayer.

September rolled his eyes. "Sure. That's why his ashes are in a wooden box and not one of your fancy urns."

The headmaster ignored his comment. "That being said, with new arrivals needing lodgings, I thought you would be so kind as to accommodate our young friend. Since half of your room has recently been vacated. It's for the best."

"What? Why me?" September fumed. "July has a bigger room all to herself! And there's space in the attic; shove him there."

"Now, now," Father Emilio removed his glasses, wiping them with a cloth. "July is a girl, so we can't have that. Besides, wouldn't you enjoy the company before you graduate shortly? It's for the best, young man."

The blond turned to face the boy in the chair, who was now looking at him questioningly. He wondered if the newcomer understood what they were saying. He wondered what his life was like in the days before he arrived.

"Fine." He took the boy by the arm abruptly and led him out of the office. "Let's go, newbie."

They made their way through the halls of St. Isidore and up the stairs to the kids' chambers. Once his arm was freed, the boy now known as November sat atop the untouched bed on the left side of the room.

"Where's your stuff?" September asked.

The boy looked at him with a blank expression.

September sighed. "Not a talker, are you?" He sat on the floor in front of the redhead. "Do – you – understand – English? *Parles-tu Français?*"

The boy just nodded in response.

"Fantastic," September groaned. "English it is. Where are you from? How old are you, like 4? 5? How did they find you?"

Silence.

Then, without warning, the boy began to cry. In quiet sobs, tears streamed down his cheeks as he tried to wipe them away with a sleeve.

"Wait, hold on!" September jumped to his feet in a panic. "Stop crying! Why are you crying? Was it something I said?"

The redhead covered his face with his hands and continued to sob. In between short gasps of air, September was able to make out the words "want" and "mama."

He rubbed the back of his head, uncertain. "I – I know, but mama is gone, probably. This is your home now." He sat on the bed next to the crying child, who flinched away in response.

The answer was evidently not satisfactory, as November just cried harder.

September swore under his breath. "Goddamn kids. What can I do? What do you want? Do you like chocolate?"

Without waiting for an answer, he pulled a hidden compartment out from the floorboards, revealing a small stash of candy.

The crying eased up for a moment.

"Only your predecessor and I know about this collection, so zip it, *capisce*?" He held out a chocolate bar to the boy.

Hesitantly, November took the chocolate, wiping the tears from his eyes

September sighed in relief. "That's better. No more crying. It's annoying." He sat back down, taking some chocolate for himself and concealing the stash once more.

The redhead nibbled on the chocolate, watching the other intently without saying a word.

"Stop staring at me like that," September said, "it's creepy. Anyway, now that you stopped crying, what's your name?"

The boy sniffed. "November?"

"No, I know that." September said. "I mean your real name. Before you forget it."

November hesitated. "Not allowed."

September scoffed, "They indoctrinated you that quick, huh? I'll tell you mine. It's the best way to make sure that someone remembers who you are – were – before you got here. My name is Misha."

The boy fiddled the with chocolate bar wrapper. After a long pause, he exhaled a trembling breath and cautiously said:

"Noël."

"Nice to meet you, Noël," said Misha, studying his face. "I didn't notice before, but you have a lot of freckles. Like stars in the sky."

Noël stared back with wide green eyes. "You have long hair. Like a girl."

"Watch it," Misha warned. "You'll want me on your side in here. Don't piss me off, and I'll protect you. Deal?"

The 15th Generation November hung his head in apology. "Okay."

- Niagara Falls, ON. February 18, 2014 -

The cozy tearoom behind the bookcase in the *Queen of Spades* café was quiet, save for the sound of a spoon stirring sugar in a teacup.

Noa hoped that he misheard, but as he looked to the unbranded black laptop in front of him to the man sitting across from him, he thought better.

He had already been silent for too long. Did he seem suspicious? Noa opened his mouth but then promptly closed it again. He removed his glasses, pretending to clean them on the sleeve of his sweater.

"What do you mean by 'hack,' exactly?" Noa asked finally.

"I didn't mean to put you on the spot," Sebastian said.

You definitely did, the young agent thought, putting his glasses back on.

"Consider it a test," he said, placing the teacup in its saucer.

Noa hesitantly opened the foreign laptop. "Of my security program or my hacking abilities?" As the words left his mouth, he realized it was—

"Both," Sebastian smiled.

Hiding his face behind the computer screen, Noa's mind went into overdrive. If he had his government software, he could easily hack into the system – but even without it, he could make do. Should he, though? What was the Niagara Co. boss testing for?

He rubbed his eyes, suppressing a yawn. "Okay," he said. "Give me some time."

"Certainly," Sebastian took a book off a nearby shelf. "All the time you need."

"Got it."

Sebastian shut his book, setting it aside. "That was faster than I anticipated." He checked his watch. "Thirty minutes?"

Noa looked down apologetically. He stalled as much as he could; truthfully, he could have finished in fifteen. "I'm sorry, sir. I guess it was not as secure as I thought. I can power it down immediately. Or, if you'd like, I can look into some password-protected closed-circuit options for an upgraded—"

"Where did you learn to do this?" Sebastian interrupted, turning the laptop to watch the Parlor's video feed.

"Self-taught, sir!" Noa said with a hint of pride. "I'm better at hacking into security systems than making them."

"Evidently," Sebastian said, scrolling through the windows of code on the screen.

Noa waited anxiously. His eyes drifted to the book at Sebastian's side, stomach instantly dropping upon reading the title: *Merchant of Venice*. He turned his attention instead to Sebastian himself.

He was no expert in men's fashion, but he was certain the Niagara Co.'s boss spared no expense. Every time they met, he wore a quality suit, as black as the color of his hair. Noa felt severely underdressed in his jeans and sweater. And he noticed that beaded necklace again, obscured by the collar of his shirt.

Noa desperately want to ask him some questions. "Did I pass?"

Sebastian closed the programs. "Well done. First, I'd like you to shut off the video monitoring of the Parlor. Second, can you repeat what you've done here for another location?"

Intrigued, Noa opened his own laptop again. "I don't see why not. Where?"

"Manhattan."

Unable to contain himself, Noa asked, "Also one of your locations?"

"Yes," Sebastian confirmed. "I suppose you could say it's a storage facility. It has a camera monitoring system, to which I have access."

"I'm confused," Noa said. "If you have access to it, then why do you want me to hack it?"

"Humor me." Sebastian opened the remote security view on his computer. A grainy camera display appeared on his screen, revealing stacks of boxes and various containers, as well as two armed men in suits. The facility resembled an endless underground garage.

"I'll try," Noa said. "What's the address? Also, if you know the software developer, it'll be much faster."

"133 West 71st Street," Sebastian said. "The company was Circuitex, I believe."

Noa pulled his own laptop closer, opening a series of programs. While he filtered through the password cracker, he peered over the screen across the table. "Do you have a lot of business in Manhattan?"

Sebastian leaned back in the chair. "Why do you ask? Are you interested in visiting?"

"No, no," the redhead backtracked. "I was just wondering. I mean, you're called the *Niagara Company*, but..." he thought about how to pose his question nonchalantly: "you clearly operate beyond Niagara. Right?"

"Certainly," the other man said, without elaborating.

Noa bit down his frustration. "I, um, saw the waterfall vault the other day. With Nick. That was so cool," he said, not completely dishonestly. "Does this Manhattan place contribute to that?"

"Good question," Sebastian said. "I consider it more of a legacy business."

"Legacy?" Noa echoed. "What do you mean by—oh. Hang on, I just got the password. I should be able to get into the network now."

Sebastian rested his elbow on the table, glancing at his computer's original camera feed of the storage facility.

"Huh." Noa blinked a few times, squinting at the screen. "That's weird."

"What is it?" Sebastian asked, watching the back of Noa's laptop.

"Are you sure you're getting a live view on your end?"

"It's timestamped with the current date and time," Sebastian said, checking his monitor. "Why?"

"Because" Noa turned his laptop around, "they don't match."

Sebastian stiffened.

It was empty.

He hit the table with a sudden impact, causing Noa to jump in his seat slightly.

"I knew it. Of all the places to rob," he scoffed under his breath. "Alright, Noa. Let's go."

"Where are we going?" Noa asked, nerves building again. He could tell someone wronged Sebastian, and he was catching onto a trend of what happened to those people.

The other man didn't respond. He stood from the table, sliding the black computer back into its hiding place and activating a switch that opened the bookcase doorway to the private dining room.

Noa grabbed his belongings and hurried after him to find Mike already waiting in the car outside.

"Ready, Boss?" Mike greeted with a friendly grin.

"Get the team together," Sebastian responded firmly.

"Ten-four!" Mike held the door for him and then waved at Noa. "Good meetin', then?"

Noa wasn't so sure. The drive back across the border was silent. He stared at the back of the passenger seat, wishing he could have asked more questions.

SIXTEEN

ST. ISIDORE: PART V. DELUGE

- Monaco. Winter, 2003 -

July found September in the courtyard, sitting up against the ornate fountain, now extinguished for the winter months. Six-year-old November was studying a textbook on a bench nearby.

"Is it true?" July demanded, more as a statement and less as a question. She planted herself in front of September, blocking the sunlight in which he was lounging.

September opened one eye lazily. "That depends. Will my saying 'yes' make you go away? In which case, yes, of course, whatever you want."

July crossed her arms in an attempt to appear more threatening. At seventeen, the teenage girl's main intimidation tactics involved her close relationships with St. Isidore staff and a menacing glare.

"I'm graduating next week," she said.

"Congratulations," said September flatly, closing both eyes again. "*Bon chance.*"

"Shut up," she spat. "Is it true that you were meant to graduate *last year?*"

"I'm sure I don't know what you're talking about," he said. "Clearly you're graduating first since you're the smartest. Go you."

"Don't mock me," July said bitterly. "It's bad enough being second but being second to *you* is—is just... And for what? For *him?*" She gestured at November's bench with a flip of her hand.

September ignored her insinuation but glanced at the redhead.

"Hey, November," he called out, "I'll meet you in the library. It's getting cold."

The boy looked up from his book and nodded obediently, leaving the bench and heading inside the doors of St. Isidore's.

"So, you admit it, then." July said. "You're purposely staying back for the kid."

"Why do you care?" September demanded.

"You're wasting your potential!" she raised her voice. "It's insulting. What would November think? The original November."

September's face went blank. "...what?"

July tightened her scarf, looking around. "Not here. Follow me."

She hurried out of the courtyard and past the orphanage gates, towards the harbor.

September followed reluctantly. They crept up seventy steps in awkward silence, to the top of a rickety lighthouse.

September grazed his hand along the crumbling bricks of Lucciana's interior. "Why here?"

"What do you think happened to November?" she asked firmly.

His breath caught in his throat. "What do you mean? He... he died. Bee sting."

"Anaphylactic shock, that's what Emilio told you?" July put her hands in the pockets of her coat. "You believe it?"

"I saw him—" September looked away briefly, stepping back towards the window. "I saw his face. He suffocated."

"More than one way to die of asphyxiation," she stated matter-of-factly. "Strangulation. Poison. Carbon monoxide. *Drowning*—"

September kicked over the window-side crate, sending it splintering across the floor. "What the *fuck* are you talking about?"

July didn't react. "I hear things. In Emilio's quarters. From the Sisters. There were concerns about your friendship with November."

September stayed silent, struggling to steady his breathing.

July went on. "Concerns that you might let yourself fall behind to stay together. Concerns that you, top of the 14th Generation, a St. Isidore prodigy with incredible potential, might—"

"No," he said.

July peered at him curiously. "No?"

September was facing away, fixated on the shattered crate.

"No," he repeated, barely above a whisper. *They wouldn't go so far...* "No."

The girl shrugged. "I don't have proof beyond a reasonable doubt. But, on the day November died, I overheard Sister Mary and Father Emilio talking. Mary found something in his belongings and Emilio told her to get rid of it."

From her pocket, July retrieved a small wooden box. A 6-letter combination lock held it shut.

"I was on garbage duty that day," she said. "Found this in Mary's trash, but I haven't been able to open it. Now that I'm leaving, figured you might as well have it."

Eyes burning, September snatched the box from her hands. "You had this *for over a year?*"

She shrugged. "I thought there might be treasure inside, or something. Wouldn't you have done the same?"

Without a second thought, September input the letters that clicked the lock open.

July lifted a brow, "Who's Aurora?"

"Shut up." September flung the little box open, taking out its sole contents with trembling hands: a piece of notebook paper.

He stepped a few feet away from July's prying eyes.

Dear ~~Misha September~~ Misha,

*I'm sorry. Sorry you waited around for me. Sorry I'm leaving like this. Remember our plan? ~~I think~~ It's for the best if I go alone. You should stay. Graduate and become the most powerful mogul they've ever seen! Never give them a penny. I'm sorry you're finding out this way. If I told you in person, you'd stop me. ~~I want this~~ **It's for the best.***

~~I'll try~~ I'll think of you when I sail the Gibraltar Strait and into the Atlantic, up to the North and Baltic sea, like we planned, and dock in the Neva river. To see the Aurora. When I was five, I nearly drowned.

I have been terrified of water ever since.

But you have to dive despite the risk of drowning, right? This is me diving.

~~If this is goodbye, if I don't make it,~~ if I never see you again...

Please, remember me.

Your friend,

Sebastian

The words swirled in a typhoon of ink behind his eyes. Plan? Dive? Was this a farewell letter or a suicide note?

September grounded himself, fixating on two odd repetitions.

It's for the best. Where had he heard that before? He looked up, a vice grip tightening around his heart, to see July watching him inquisitively.

The Headmaster. They did this. His friend would never choose to leave him. Willingly set foot on a sailboat. His friend who drowned even in his dreams.

September's hand curled into a fist around the letter. They pushed Sebastian to the brink, knowing he would take the final step.

Thursday, January 23rd, was a winter's day like any other in 2003. Perhaps more unfortunate than others that preceded it, perhaps not.

On January 23rd, the well-traveled Bahamian cruise ship, *HMS Wind Song,* had sunk 1,600 fathoms beneath French Polynesian waters.

On January 23rd, 12 billion kilometers from earth, Jupiter-bound spacecraft *Pioneer 10* lost radio communications with humanity.

On January 23rd, boarding an Italy-bound train, 16-year-old September fled St. Isidore's Home for Extraordinary Children and never looked back.

Realizing the fate that awaited November's successor if he stayed behind for him, he had made up his mind. There would be no graduation. No Isidorian placement. He wouldn't give them that satisfaction.

He would rather run than live up to Emilio's vision of his 'potential.' At this age, rational thinking was not September's forte.

He managed to sneak past the train patrol in Ventimiglia and pressed on, recklessly, through Genoa until ultimately getting thrown out in Milan's grand central station with a stern warning.

After five and half hours of anxious cabin-hopping, September slid down to the floor in a corner of Milano Centrale, drowning out the waves of commuters flooding the elegant halls.

He had barely €100, which he managed to pilfer from the pockets of St. Isidore staff, and no rhyme or reason to his journey. He considered trying his luck in Russia, but just the thought dredged up unwelcome shadows of quelled memories.

He couldn't possibly return, to either home. So, what now?

Wander aimlessly until I starve?

An automated announcement broke through his haze.

"Signore e signori. Il treno uno-uno-zero-nove a Venezia Mestre parte tra quindici minuti dal binario quarantatre. Ladies and gentlemen. Train 1109 to Venice Mestre leaves in fifteen minutes from platform forty-three."

His head shot up. Suddenly he knew why he traveled in this direction. Why he made the last-minute decision to don the urn-side rosary from his bedroom drawer.

He had 15 minutes to find his way to train number 1109 on platform 43. Plenty of time. Before making his way to the trains, September followed a rowdy American family into a minimarket near the ticket booths.

While they overwhelmed the cashier with a counter piled-high with their traveling essentials, September quietly slipped out with two hidden items in his jacket pocket.

He got on train 1109 with a minute to spare, feigning worry that his parents went ahead without him and he got lost – but they have his ticket. He'll show it during patrol check, of course, but he needs to get on *now* as they're seven cars away.

September went cabin-to-cabin, avoiding detection, as the train peacefully exited Milan. When it approached Verona, September awoke from a restless nap to the sound of guards entering his car.

He studied his surroundings.

The guards were making their way up from the south end of the car, verifying tickets. September and his immediate neighbors were in the middle. An elderly French woman in front of him was asleep. Two teens by the window were also asleep, both dark-haired Italian brothers, it seemed.

To his left, a group of four foreigners – a family from India. Three asleep, one staring out the window.

September was perfectly out of place.

He rose from his seat, making sure to glance back at the patrolmen for a delayed moment, before quickly ducking into the bathroom. Removing the items that he snatched from the station store, September locked the door and got to work.

About thirty minutes later, after disposing of the evidence, he returned to his seat. The passengers had gone back to sleep. He gently woke the brother by the forward-facing window.

"*Scusi,*" he said in Italian, "if you're going to sleep, could I sit by the window? I would love to watch the landscape."

The teenager looked at him with some drowsy confusion, but muttered *"si, si"* and traded seats. September removed his jacket and took his place by the window just as one of the guards returned.

The uniformed man stopped near September's quadrant of seats. He checked his notepad, perplexed.

"Son," he said to the dozing teenage boy. "Can I see your ticket?"

The boy groaned. "I showed you already! Here, god." He pulled it out of his pocket.

The guard furrowed his brows. September carefully kept his gaze fixed on the moon.

"Did you seen a blonde young lady go through here, longer hair, about your age?" asked the guard. "About half an hour ago."

The boy yawned, half-listening. "No, man. No blondies here. Let me sleep, there's only like three stops till Venice."

Apologizing, the guard left. September leaned his head against the window and, lulled by the gentle rocking of the rails, fell asleep.

September's primary motivation in leaving St. Isidore's was to prevent Noël from suffering as his friend Sebastian suffered.

His secondary motivation was to inflict some kind of damage upon the Home's reputation or credibility by leaving.

He was also motivated to honor his dear friend's memory by making a difference in his own, small way.

However, motivations quickly leave one's mind when

poverty is a very possible and threatening reality. September's thoughts had turned instead to survival. Although he could have always returned to Monaco, his pride would never allow it.

It did not take long for September to ascertain the sheer power of the criminal underworld – especially in Italy. It fascinated him and lured him into its clutches with the promise of riches and prosperity. He made it his goal to join the mafia.

This would not have come as a great surprise to the headmasters of St. Isidore's. September's file, in addition to his high potential for success, profiled him with a predisposition towards politics and business.

Now, it should be known that, despite what it may claim, St. Isidore's Home does not raise exceptional members of society. It raises brilliant children into adults that stop at nothing to achieve their objectives. If they're patient and tough, someday their pain will be useful.

Such qualities are meant to help create the world's best citizens, but they can also be applied to entirely different situations.

For September, it was not a question of *if,* but rather of *how.* As with all Isidore alumni, he considered no resource too small or too precious to use to succeed. Which is why, to him, his body was just another resource.

After a few weeks of gathering information, he had his target.

Gio Rossini was his name in the underworld. A bald man in his late thirties, he was a top-dog in the Mala del Brenta – the Venetian mafia. An unruly man with a short fuse, Rossini had a vision for expansion but was held back by traditional values.

September formulated a risky plan. After tracking down

Rossini's crew, he posed as a clueless runaway and 'accidentally' stumbled upon his base. When he was captured and thrown down to Rossini's feet, September pleaded for the man to spare his life in exchange for his complete devotion.

He added that he would do anything so long as Rossini didn't kill him. *Anything.*

Rossini considered him with an amused and lecherous smile. "What's your name, *ragazzo?*"

September did not skip a beat. "Sebastian." Then, deciding on a whim to keep a piece of his monthly identity, added, "Nové. Sebastian Nové"

Unsurprisingly, Rossini accepted. September had done his research and knew that the mobster had a revolting penchant for underage boys.

Everything about Gio Rossini disgusted him. The way his too-strong cologne smelled; the way his voice boomed too loudly when he laughed; the way he didn't bother wiping the blood off his shoes after a kill; the way his hands felt on the boy's skin; the way his breath was too hot up against his neck; the way he— well, you get the picture.

Little by little, September ceased to exist. Sebastian Nové took over.

Rossini took him everywhere like a lapdog. Sebastian grew accustomed to faking smiles and accepting wine, accompanying his boss with unwavering loyalty. He drew people in with his charm and kept them entranced with those fierce eyes.

After some time, Sebastian's resolve began to pay off.

By seventeen, he was proving to be an asset to the Mala del Brenta, bringing in valuable information and even more valuable clients. And thanks to Rossini's place on the hierarchy and his favoritism towards Sebastian, he quickly rose in the ranks.

Yes, he was young, but he was extraordinarily sharp. He encouraged Rossini's plans of expansion, to nearby islands and Venetian mainland, eventually persuading him to branch out to New York. Since Sebastian was so fluent in English, he was more than willing to help.

By the age of twenty, Sebastian commanded subdivisions in Manhattan, while Rossini was busy with the matters in Italy. With his boss was abroad, Sebastian built up a loyalty and preference to himself over his superior in the land of the free.

Rumors of Sebastian Nové started to spread. A fair-skinned, well-read foreigner with unnaturally dark hair and intense eyes the color of a cloudless winter sky. An indiscernible accent and unrelenting charisma. Youthful and fearless. The Millennial Tycoon. Soon, his popularity overtook Rossini's.

COMING SOON...

The story continues in...

THE HELL'S HALF ACRE TRADE
Part Two of the St. Isidore Series

A mysterious person from the past returns. A tearful reunion. A mistake. A betrayal.

Will Agent Noa Sinclair discover the Niagara Company's secrets before they discover his? Find out in the thrilling sequel!

EXCERPT FROM HELL'S HALF ACRE TRADE

INITIATION

A forceful winter storm raged outside the windows of the Polar Parlor's second floor office, flurries of scattered snowflakes hurrying in every direction on gales of river wind. Sebastian was leaning up against the mahogany desk, unreadable expression on his face.

Noa sat in one of the office chairs, computer in his lap. He watched as the other members of the Niagara Co. entered the room.

"Hey, sugar," Elli came in first, taking a seat on the windowpane. Nick, who sat in a chair on the other side of the room, soon followed.

Mike rushed inside, dusting snow off his hat, "What's going on, Boss? Are we under attack?" He took a seat across from the desk, beside Noa.

"I reckon we'd know if we were under attack," Elli said. Then, hesitantly, "we're not, are we? I don't like that look, Bassie."

Sebastian exhaled. "I suppose you could call it an attack of sorts."

The woman from the Bella Luna alleyway trailed in last, after Mike. Noa now knew her name to be Lucy. She said nothing, taking her post by the window next to Elli. She wore a long trench coat and a surprisingly bright pink scarf, tied snugly around her neck.

Nick sat up, all ears. "Manhattan?"

Sebastian gave a slight nod. "Noa, if you would."

Tense from nerves and the five pairs of eyes awaiting his next move, Noa hurriedly opened his laptop and placed it on the desk for the others to see the screen. The grainy footage of an empty storeroom filled the display.

Elli gasped, "We've been robbed? Either that, or you're finally doing spring cleaning as I keep suggesting."

Mike leaned in, looking at the monitor. "But this place didn't store anything special, did it? Who would rob it?"

"It was Giovanni Rossini, wasn't it?" Nick said with a snarl. "That piece of shit."

Rossini? Noa searched the archives of his recent memory. He recalled seeing the name from his tangential investigation into the Venetian mafia while he was researching Sebastian's mysterious origins. He had crossed the ocean to New York City and controlled a large portion of the mob, at one time.

Is it the same one? Involved with Niagara Co.? Noa flinched when Sebastian's gloved hand came to rest on his shoulder.

"It was Rossini. Thanks to Noa, we can make the first move," he said.

"Way to go, hon'!" Elli smiled. "So, what now?"

Noa winced as the grip on his shoulder tightened.

"Well," Sebastian said in a low voice. "It has become clear that something must be done about him, since he is sending me this message."

Nick pounded a closed fist into his open palm. "Yes! About time. We have all that new ammo sittin' around, collecting dust – can I finally use it?"

Elli rolled her eyes, wrapping an arm around Lucy with a dramatic gesture. "Right, but there's a reason it's collecting dust. Besides, why would we send you, Nicky, when we've got this lovely lady?"

Lucy absentmindedly stroked the knitted hem of her scarf. "I can terminate him," she said in a voice that hovered just above a whisper.

Noa made an effort to keep his reactions to a minimum. He heaved a mental sigh of relief when Sebastian released his shoulder and went behind the desk.

"Let's park that for now," he said, taking a seat. "Elli, who's watching the Parlor at the moment?" Sebastian locked eyes with her for a second.

"Mike said it was an emergency— ah." Elli hummed in confirmation. She let go of Lucy, turning her attention to the redhead. "Noa, sugar, can you cover the counter for a bit?"

"Now? But I—" he protested only to be cut off by Elli's finger suddenly pressed against his mouth. She kneeled down beside him.

"Now. Thanks, hon'." She poked him on the nose gently.

Noa looked around the room. Defeated, he packed up his laptop and left with a sulk. As he shut the door behind him, Mike called out:

"Don't eavesdrop this time, kiddo."

Behind the frosted purple and white counter of the Polar Parlor, Noa stared at the falling snow beyond the glass and fumed.

How he would have loved to be a fly on the wall of the conversation taking place upstairs! Granted, it didn't seem to have anything to do with insider trading, but still it was an opportunity to see how they operated. How they plot revenge – how often can one witness *that*?

Oh, no. Noa blinked, halting his own train of thought. He wasn't excited by this, was he?

No, of course not, he reasoned, *I'm just investigating.* Clearly, they're planning something illegal. He glanced at the staff-access door. Something undoubtedly illegal, devious, and *cool— no!*

Stop thinking like that! Noa shook his head subconsciously, leaving the counter and starting to pace the length of the Parlor's floor.

What are they planning? He gazed up at the ceiling, decorated with its twine-hung silver snowflakes, while pacing back and forth.

Nick mentioned new ammunition. The quiet woman, Lucy, said she would kill outright. A gang of criminals, nothing less. Noa repeated the fact to himself, finding that it would occasionally slip his mind.

How could it not? Most of his time with the Niagara Co., to date, has been spent helping Elli, or joining her for a card game with Mike. Even the few interactions he's had with Sebastian have been friendly.

They treated each other as friends. Or rather, as family. Noa felt the unspoken trust between each of the members in the room upstairs; he yearned for a similar connection.

He stopped pacing. Not with *them,* surely.

Noa sat at a pink table and groaned, semi-hoping a customer would enter the shop to distract him. As a last resort, he spent his idle time fixing the PecanBot.

After an agonizingly long forty-five minutes, Mike called Noa back up to the office.

ST. ISIDORE: PART VI. CASA NOVÉ

The putrid smell of gasoline and smoke lingered in the air. Iron and salt. The lights, flickering, cast billowing shadows on the stained, splintering surroundings.

"I'm bigger now. I'm stronger now."

Bullet shells and bodies litter the floor. Screams and curses echo down the halls.

"This is *my* domain."

A man is pushed against a wall, fear reflecting in his eyes. A hand grabs him by the throat. He strains against it.

"Nové. How can you do this to me? After I took you in!"

A scoff.

"Please take a bow, Gio. I am your work of art." The sound of a flicked lighter.

The man shuddered at the sight before him. A beautiful, raven-haired devil with blue lightning in his eyes.

"Are you going to kill me?"

"Shouldn't I?"

"I gave you everything." It was a desperate tone. "I spoiled you rotten!"

A bitter laugh.

"Definitely rotten. You shouldn't have come here, Gio. All that glitters is not gold – didn't you know?"

"Please, just spare my life! Have mercy on me. I'll work for you."

A plea.

A consideration.

"Beg some more. I'll think about it."

ABOUT THE AUTHOR

This is Daria's first novel, published alongside its sequel, *The Hell's Half Acre Trade*.

Daria lives on the harbor front of Lake Ontario with her husband and elderly Shih Tzu, spending as much time by the water as possible. Born in Russia, she has lived most of her life in Canada.

When she is not writing or listening to Broadway show tunes, Daria works in financial consulting. Both she and her husband also enjoy travelling (outside of global pandemics). Daria's favorite destinations include Mediterranean France & Italy – what a surprise!

CPSIA information can be obtained
at www.ICGtesting.com
Printed in the USA
LVHW020208300721
694057LV00005B/684

9 798503 454598